Felicity

Alessa Maynard

Contents

Prologue : 1

Dark Night with loud thunders and heavy rain.

But Today, Sky is not only one crying.

"P-Ple-ease B-Believe me, Dad, p-please- AHHHHH"

A 13 year little boy screamed due to pain. His voice echoed through the Whole Russo Mansion. But it is deaf to all the living ears.

"YOU ARE NOTHING BUT A DISGRACE TO OUR FAMILY" His father again hit him with his leather belt, making him scream again.

But if you ask him what is more painful ?

The answer will be that Disappoint look in his Father's eyes, and that hateful look, his mother is giving to him.

Yes, He can tolerate this beatings but he can't tolerate hate from his loved ones. From his Mom. From his Dad. He always wanted to be the Best Son ever.

"D-Dad-"

"SHUT THE FUCK UP, YOU WILL NEVER CALL ME DAD, AGAIN" His dad again smacked his bare back with that leather belt.

"AHHHHH- P-Ple-ease, t-trust me, p-pleas-se , I-am i-innoc- AHHHH-HH"

"SO, YOU ARE TELLING MY SISTER IS LYING, HUH ? HOW *SMACK* DARE *SMACK* YOU *SMACK* ?" His Dad pulled his hair.

"She told me many times but I NEVER BELIEVED HER, I WAS SO FOOLISH TO TRUST YOU OVER HER. HOW FUCKING DARE YOU TO TOUCH HER-" He yelled and beat him continuously without looking at his son's condition.

"N-NO, I NEVER T-TOUCH HER, INSTEAD S-SHE T-TOUCHED M-ME-" He fell down because of very loud slap on his face.

"DARE TO SAY A WORD AGAINST MY SISTER"

He gritted his teeth, growling at his son.

Little Boy winced falling on the ground. His heart shattered into million pieces when he heard his Dad's voice. He weakly looked at his Mom only to see, her standing there with tears in her eyes.

"M-Mom" He whispered.

His Mom turned her back towards him.

Tears streaming down his cheeks.

He weakly stood up from his place and ran towards his Mom. He fell holding her leg "M-Mom p-please believe me, s-she is l-lying, s-she t-touched m-me in m-my p-pri-ivate p-part- AHHHHHHHHH" He Screamed due to pain as his Dad stepped on his bare injured back with his pointed shoes.

"YOU ARE A FUCKING BASTARD. WHY DON'T YOU JUST DIE ?" His Dad growled.

Thunder striked again.

He looked up at his Mom with tear stained face with a little hope that his Mom will trust him.

But his little hope just crushed down when his Mom said "I am really embarrassed because of you, how can you stoop so low ? You touched your own Aunt ? YOU FUCKING R-RAPE YOUR OWN AUNT ? You made her P-Pregnant ? I wish you were never born. Why didn't you die as soon as you were born ? You are nothing but a disappointment, Vincenzo. SHAME ON YOU, VINCENZO, SHAME ON YOU"

And then and there, VINCENZO RUSSO lost his Parents and his normal life...

Prologue : 2

Author's P.O.V.

9 Months Later...

A baby wrapped in a pink towel is sleeping peacefully in the crib.

She didn't even open her eyes yet.

There is no one in the room except the baby.

A door creaked as 14 year old fragile boy entered in the room.

Yes, Vincenzo Russo. 14 years Old.

Sensing someone entered in room, that little baby started crying, still not opening her eyes. Vincenzo's eyes widened. He panicked.

He immediately rushed towards the crib.

But before he could even touch her, door opened again revealing nothing but a woman in her 30s. She has a glare on her face. A nurse supporting her.

She came towards the crib and glared at the baby, but immediately smiled seeing nurse.

"Sister, can you give us a minute ?"

Nurse nodded and left.

That woman turned towards Vincenzo.

She smirked.

"Ooo Little Boy, how are you ?"

Vincenzo glared at her.

"Angry huh ? Well, let me tell you one thing, this little thing here is yours. Take this. And remember one thing, if you ever opened your mouth against me, I will kill your daughter" She growled.

Door opened suddenly as a couple entered.

Glare on Women's face disappeared as it was never there before, instead she has tears in her eyes.

"Shaira" That man immediately came towards her.

"Are you ok ?" He asked her worriedly.

That Woman who is now named as Shaira sniffled "N-No Alessio, I-I c-can't even call my d-daughter m-mine, A-Alessio. S-She is a p-product of R-Rape-" Shaira cried on Alessio's shoulder. He rubbed her back glaring at his son, Vincenzo.

Yes, Alessio Russo is Vincenzo's Father.

"Laura Take her out" Alessio told his wife who nodded in response.

Shaira sobbed but secretly smirked at Vincenzo. Who in response just stood there numb and emotionless.

"Listen You little bastard, Don't. Ever. Tell. Anyone. That. She. Is Shaira's. Daughter. Otherwise, I will make her life hell just like I am making yours." Alessio growled.

"And anyways, she is your dirt. However, you know, when she will grew up, she will hates you too. Afterall you raped her Mom" Alessio smirked and left the room without looking at that little baby.

All this time that little baby is walling her heart out. Vincenzo looked at her.

His eyes watered. He felt on his knees and started crying.

He looked at that little baby's face.

She is so innocent.

What's her fault ?

Why everyone started hating her already ?

Why everyone started threatening her ?

What she did to them ?

Why she is dragged in all these ?

He sobbed his heart out.

He was innocent too.

What's his fault ?

What's his fault when his Aunt kept touching him ?

What's his fault when His Dad always leave him with his Aunt ?

What's his fault when his Aunt threatened him to kill his parents ?

What's his fault when she raped him ?

It's not like he didn't try to protect himself. He tried. He tried his best but how could a 13 year old fight with a lady whom he thinks of as a Mother ?

Why he was dragged in all these ?

He was innocent too, right ?

Tears never stopped from his eyes. He wants to hold that little baby but can't.

Why ? Because he was scared ? What if she will get hurt ? What if she will hates him too ? His heart dropped at this.

She started crying loud like telling him to pick her up.

Vincenzo slowly picked her in his arms and the joy he felt in his heart is ETHEREAL.

He forgot all his pain, miseries everything for a second as he just felt an unknowing joy crept in his heart.

He slowly brings her close to his chest and she immediately stopped her crying. Vincenzo's eyes widened.

"Wow Vince"

He heard a voice but can't take off his eyes from his Little girl.

And almost immediately he is surrounded by two little boys on his either side.

"She stopped crying Vince" One boy said shocked.

"Vinceeeee what are you holding ? What is this ?" Another little boy said.

Vincenzo chuckled at his little brother's question.

"She is little girl, Ric and she is going to live with us" Vincenzo replied to his youngest 10 year old brother Riccardo Russo.

Riccardo widened his eyes.

"Girl ?" He leaned near Vincenzo's ears and whispered "She will poop, Vince"

"Fool, My madam said All living things poop" His another brother re-marked.

"Yes, Ric, he is right and Sal, don't call your brother 'Fool'" Vincenzo said behaving maturely to his 12 year second youngest brother Salvatore Russo.

"Ok Vince. But what are we gonna call her ?" Salvatore asked him.

"Heyyy what about Poopy Princess ?" Riccardo squealed.

"No Ric, we can't" Salvatore instructed.

Vincenzo chuckled. He zoned out from his brothers' argument and looked at the little bundle of joy in his hand.

She is so soft. So cute. So beautiful.

Before he could even think anything else, a word left from his lips making that little girl opened her beautiful doe eyes.

"Bella"

Chapter 1

----

1 2 Years Later...

"Bells, wake up baby" A hand caressed a little girl's hair trying to wake her up from her deep slumber.

She didn't even budge a muscle.

"Bells, wake up" He shook her slightly.

The said girl stirred in her sleep murmuring some incoherent words, she turned other Side.

That Man chuckled.

He placed a kiss on her forehead and again shook her a little.

"Baby, wake up, you don't wanna go to the beach today, hmm ?"

The brown eyes of that little 12 year old girl jerked open as she heard a word 'beach'.

"I am Up, Sal, I am up." She said coming in sitting position.

Salvatore chuckled and ruffled her already bad messy hair.

"Go and get fresh. Come down for breakfast" He smiled at her.

She whinned.

"I am tired, Sal"

He playfully narrowed his eyes.

"Oh really ?"

She nodded with a pout.

"Oh no, then we have to cancel today's plan, sad but it's ok, you are tired so-"

"No No I am not tired, I was just joking, Sal, look I am running" She said sprinting towards bathroom.

Salvatore Laughed heartily seeing her antics.

He shook his head and left towards the Kitchen. He came downstairs and immediately a glare set in his eyes.

"RIC, WHAT ARE YOU DOING ?"

The said brother looked up and shrugged "practicing"

Riccardo Russo is dribbling his ball in living room, breaking two vases in process.

Salvatore pinched his bridge of nose in frustration "IN FUCKING LIV-ING ROOM ?"

"Calm down Old man" Riccardo sighed.

"CLEAN EVERYTHING IN 5 FUCKING MINUTES OTHERWISE FORGET ABOUT YOUR BREAKFAST" Salvatore yelled and stormed towards kitchen.

Riccardo sighed seeing all the mess he made.

"5 minutes ? Not possible" He sighed looking around.

"Nancyyyyyy"

"Yes Ric ?" A lady in her 40s stood infront of him.

"Nancy please help me" Riccardo pouted.

Nancy, their maid chuckled and nodded.

"Ok"

They started cleaning their messy living room.

But turned their head hearing anklet sound.

"Riccyyy" She beamed and jumped in Riccardo's arms. He caught her in his embrace and hugged her tightly.

"What's my Baby girl is doing ?" He asked in his deep voice.

"Hugging my favourite brother" Bella squealed when he tickled her sides.

"Good, you are learning well, baby girl" Riccardo smirked.

Bella giggled loudly.

"BELLS COME FOR BREAKFAST" A Voice boomed through the mansion from the kitchen.

"COMING SAL" She yelled back.

"Go Go otherwise we will wake up that sleepy Beast" Riccardo said keeping her on her feet and patted her bum.

She giggled and ran towards the kitchen.

"I am here, Sal" She said smiling to Salvatore, who is busy in serving the food.

"Oh wow. What that Stinky Pig said ?"

Bella giggled.

"Nothing Sal, he told me to go and eat my breakfast" She said showing her dimples.

"Oh yeah, I totally believe you" Sal said sarcastically minding his own business.

"You should believe her, Sallyy" Riccardo voice heard. Salvatore sighed.

"Shut up Ric, and eat your breakfast" Salvatore scolded him who in response shrugged.

"Where is Viny, Sal ?" Bella asked.

"You know him, Babes" Sal raised his eyebrow playfully. Bella giggled.

"Go and bring him, please Bells" Sal winked at her.

She nodded running towards his office.

She knocked on the door.

Instead of 'Come in', she heard a door opened and immediately squealed in shocked when suddenly she was being lifted.

"Vinnyyyyyy" She beamed in excitement hugging Vincenzo.

He chuckled and kissed on her forehead and cheeks, before holding her securely in his arms.

"Why didn't you come down Vinny ?" Bella asked.

"If I had come down, would you have come to call me up ? What's the fun in that ?" Vince winked at her.

Bella playfully glared at him.

He tickled at her. She let out a fit of giggles. Both brothers turned their head towards the source of giggles.

They looked at each other with a hearty smile.

He set Bella down, who sits beside him.

And they started eating breakfast joking, making fun of each other, with laughs and giggles.

"When we are going Sal ?" Bella frowned.

"Where are we going Sally ?" Riccardo asked.

"First of all don't call me that, and second, not we *pointing at all of them* only we *pointing at Bella and then himself* are going to a Beach" He completed with smug look on his face.

Vincenzo straightened his back. While Riccardo looks betrayed.

"Babygirl~" He whinned.

"Stop it Ric" Sal scolded him.

"But Sal, I also wanna join" Ric pouted.

Salvatore rolled his eyes.

"No means No. You had lots of work. Go and complete it, Ric" Salvatore scolded him. He huffed and started eating breakfast silently.

"Be Safe, Sal" Vince mumbled to his younger brother. Salvatore kept his hand on Vincenzo's hand and nod his head with an assuring smile.

Vincenzo looked at Bella. She completed her breakfast.

"Go Bells, get ready, Sal will take you"

"Ok Vinny" She said and sprinted towards her room.

"Always a runner" Salvatore chuckled.

Vincenzo turned towards his younger brother.

"Sal, take bodyguards with you. Call me if anything happens, hmm ?" Vince said dead serious. Hint of worry can clearly be seen from his voice.

"Don't worry Vince. I will take care of her" Sal said smiling.

"And you ? You should take care of yourself too" Vince said again seriously.

"He is old ass man. No one is going to kidnap him, Vince" Riccardo muttered under his breath.

Salvatore sighed in frustration.

"Told him to shut his fucking mouth otherwise I am disowning him" He complained to Vince.

"You ? You are going to disown me ? Did you even see your face in the mirror ?" Riccardo scoffed.

"Yes and it's better than your ugly ass face" Salvatore retorted.

"Oh that's why you are still single" Riccardo smirked.

"Like you are married" Salvatore rolled his eyes.

"Lots of girls have fallen for me. Girls worship the land on which I walk" Riccardo boasted.

Vincenzo sighed and shook his head.

Brothers and their non-ending arguments.

His head snapped towards the stairs when he heard anklet sound.

There she is !

His Baby, His world. His Daughter. His Bella.

To Be Continued...

I was going to update on Saturday but now as I think You guys are really waiting so, I decided that I will update it today only. So here, it is. Tell me if you like this chapter or not ?

So Do you like their relations with each other ?

Do you like Bella ?

She will be a little sweetheart so please don't hate her or her nature.

 Vote and Comment

I will meet you on Saturday till then stay safe, take care and Love Yourself .

Byee Byee... Luv ya .

Published : 12 July 2023.

Total Words : 1129 words .

Chapter 2

"I am here" Bella beamed, ascending stairs.

They looked at her.

She hoped down the last stair with a comb in her hand.

She is in floral print wide leg Cami jumpsuit.

"Vinny How am I looking ?" She said looking down her jumpsuit grinning.

"Gorgeous as always Bells" Vince smiled.

"But I don't know what to do with my hair" Bella pouted.

"Keep it open, Babygirl. It suits you" Riccardo winked.

"Okk" She said and started combing her hair.

"Sal Take care" Vincenzo said seriously, to which Salvatore rolled his eyes, but nodded nonetheless.

"I am telling you. Tell him to Take me with him. I will protect my babygirl and this old man here" Riccardo said seriously.

"No Ric. Let them go." Vincenzo said with finalty in his voice.

"I am doneee. Let's go Sal" Bella said holding Salvatore's hand. Salvatore smiled at her and they left.

Time Skip...

"Let's go Babes" Salvatore said holding her hand. She is practically jumping in her place, unable to contain her excitement.

"Calm down, Babes" Salvatore chuckled at her excitement.

"Let's gooo Sallyyyy" Salvatore chuckled and they crossed the road.

Here, they came on beach and Salvatore sat on Deck chair while Bella started making a sand castle.

They both are busy enjoying their time when suddenly group of 5 boys came there.

They all are in only shorts and with a bare upper body.

Siblings didn't mind them until Salvatore felt someone's gaze.

He looked at them only to see they are staring at Bella.

Salvatore clenched his jaw and glared at them.

One of them saw Salvatore's glare and immediately avoided his gaze. He turned towards his friends and whispered something. They all looked at him and then started avoiding Salvatore's gaze.

Soon enough, Those boys left.

"Sal, Let's go in water. I wanna swim" Bella said turning towards Salvatore.

Immediately, a smile broke through his lips "ok let's go"

They get ready and jumped in water. They played many games in water, they played volleyball on the beach and enjoyed their time.

It was nearly evening.

"Sal, I am hungry" Bella told him.

"Let's go to there" He told her pointing towards a small restaurant.

"Ok, Let's race. Who will reach there first will eat two icecream, ok ?" Bella told him smirking. He looked amused.

"Ok" He agreed.

"On the count of 3, okk ?" She asked coming in race position.

"Okk" He said copying her actions.

"Get, Set, Go~" She said sprinting towards the restaurant.

Salvatore stood there dumbfounded. He thought she will count till 3 but here she ? She just ran away. He shook his head following her.

On the half way through, he picked her up from her waist with his one hand and ran towards the restaurant. She giggled feeling tickles. His heart melt hearing those adorable giggles.

They reach the restaurant.

"Welcome Sir, Miss, please have a seat" Waiter welcomed them.

Salvatore set her on her feet and they choose their table.

"What do you want to eat Babes ?" Salvatore asked her handing her menu.

"Cream Cheese tortilla Wraps" She smiled.

"How can I help you Sir ?" A waiter approached them.

"One Creamy cheese tortilla Wrap and one veg grilled sandwich and what do you wanna drink, Bells ?" He turned towards Bella.

"Umm Water is ok"

"So water it is" Salvatore ordered.

Waiter nodded everything in his notepad and left.

"So Bells, your school is going to start soon, So Nervous or excited ?" Salvatore asked her keeping his both elbows on the table.

"Don't know Sal. I am quite nervous actually" Bella said seriously.

"Why tho ?" Salvatore asked her worriedly.

"I don't know what if I can't make friends here ?" Bella told him sadly.

"You can Bells. You are amazing. No one is going to deny your friendship, trust me" Salvatore reassured her.

"But Salvatore, why Vinny changed my school ?" Bella pouted.

Salvatore looked at her with a sad eyes.

What was he supposed to say ?

That, her So called Biological Mom is finding her ?

Not because, she wants her daughter but only because, she wants Vincenzo's property ?

He sighed.

"Bells, you know, it was fun" Salvatore smiled.

Bella frowned "How ?"

"I mean isn't it nice to make new friends ?" He asked trying his best to make her happy.

"No Sal, it's really difficult. I don't know how to make friends. I mean I want to make friends. But, I don't want to chat with them whole day through phone" Bella said annoyed.

In previous school, she made queen bees of the school her friends and they insisted her to talk to them whole day through chat or sms or on call. If she refused them, they become upset. And Bella, being soft hearted girl, always get manipulated by those girls until Riccardo found it.

"Exactly my point, princess. They are not your friends. Friends are not those who talked with you regularly, Friends are those who will help each other in their needs even though they are talking with each other in once a month. You will always feel free with them. You can be yourself with them. Now tell me do you ever feel that with your previous friends ?" Salvatore asked her.

Bella thought for a second, before shaking her head in 'No'

"Then. What if you will get nice friends in this new school, hmm ?" He asked her smiling.

Her eyes beamed at the thought.

"Yes" She cheered. Salvatore chuckled.

"Excuse me, Sir, here is your order" Waiter approached them with tray and kept it infront of them.

He served them and left.

"Wowww this looks so yummy" Bella's eyes sparkled.

"Eat it Babes" He chuckled.

They started eating with chit chatting and teasing each other.

"Babes, seat here, I will be back" Salvatore said and stood up to go towards Washroom.

"Ok Sal" She smiled and continue eating her wraps.

Salvatore looked at their bodyguard, who in response nodded their head.

He went inside the bathroom.

He did his business and started washing his hands in basin when he heard some whispers. He was going to ignore them but a sudden name perked his interest.

"Yeah they are Russos"

"You guys are new here, you don't know what they are capable of"

"We don't want to know that, but their sister-"

"Sshhh lower your volume, I don't want to be a prey of Russos"

"Shut up, you are overreacting. That girl over, is she their sister ?"

"Yeah, she is their sister. But rumours said something else"

"What rumours ?"

"Rumours are that Eldest Russo, Vincenzo Russo raped his own aunt and that girl over there is the product of that rape"

Salvatore gritted his teeth. He clenched his fist.

How dare they talked like this for his brother ?

He will kill them.

"Wow. Whatever, that Russo girl is really hmm beautiful tho"

"She is a child for fuck sake. Stop making such comments. And this is not right. You shouldn't take girls' pictures."

"You know our business, we don't care about age. And this is business, Man. Boss will be so happy when I will tell him that I get a pictures of Russo's sister"

Salvatore's eyes darkened. A moment ago smiling Salvatore is now looking like a Monster who can hunt them just within a snap of finger.

"We will get more money by selling the pictures of Russo's girl-"

Before he could complete, a punch landed on his cheek. Due to sudden impact that boy fell down on the floor holding his bloody jaw. His eyes widened when he saw his broken teeth.

He turned his head towards the man who punched him with a glare but immediately looked scared by seeing none other than Second Eldest Russo.

"How fucking dare you ?" Salvatore gritted his teeth holding that boy's color and made him stand up.

"Heyyy leave our friend" Another one shouted but Salvatore paid no attention.

He slammed that boy on the wall behind and punched him hard on his stomach. His friends try to attack Salvatore but they made no harm.

What they even think of him ?

He is Salvatore Russo. Second Oldest Russo. He is the COO of B.R Corporations. Alongside with that he is also the owner of the gyms. He is Red Belt in Karate. He is black belt in Taekwondo. It's not hard for him to deal with those teenagers.

"I-I am s-sorry, L-Leave me" The injured boy coughed out.

Salvatore pushed him towards his friends and picked his phone.

He go through his phone and his blood boiled when he saw his Bella's Photos when she was relaxing on a beach.

He gritted his teeth and delete every single photo.

He looked at them with red raged eyes and scowled "Mess with my family and I will kill you, but mess with my Bella, I will make you beg for death"

He said and called his guard.

"Take them to the Cops and tell them they are in human traffickings except this one here" He ordered pointing towards the good guy there.

"Yes Sir" Guards bowed and took those injured boys from there.

"You come here" Salvatore called that boy.

"Y-Yes Sir" He stuttered looking down.

"What's your name ?"

"Jason Anderson" He replied.

"What's your age ?"

"19"

"Why are you with them ? It's not look like that you want to be with them ?" Salvatore interrogated.

"I-I need money for my Mom. I work for them."

"But didn't you just tell them to stop doing this business ? You are also from human trafficking-"

"No Sir, I am poor but I am not a criminal. I obviously worked for them but in their Clothings companies not in human traffickings. They always took me with them. They made me their friend forcefully. As a friend, I always told them to leave all this but they never listened" He muttered.

Salvatore nodded.

"P-Please Sir, leave them. Please I am Begging you, otherwise their fathers will fire me from their company. I-I really need money Sir, My Mom is in hospital, p-please sir" He said with joining his hands.

Salvatore thought something.

"I am not going to leave them. They ruined many girls and now they will get what they deserve."

Jason sighed but nodded his head looking down.

"Well, for you, come to the B.R Corporations tomorrow" Salvatore ended.

Jason perked up at that.

"Here take my card. Show it to the manager and he will give you your work and in which hospital your mother is admitted ?"

Jason's eyes widened in shock. Voice struck in his throat. He couldn't utter a word.

"Garcia Hospital" He whispered.

"Ok, don't worry, I will pay your bills of hospital-"

"No Sir, it's ok. I will do it. Thank you so much Sir for a job. I will highly obliged to you" Jason said with tears.

Salvatore impressed at that.

"Ok, Come tomorrow on time. Remember, We Russos are very punctual" Salvatore patted his back.

"Lying" A voice said from behind.

Salvatore turned around towards the voice only to see Bella standing there with hands on her hips, glaring at him. She is standing outside of Men's Bathroom.

Salvatore widened his eyes and washed his hand cleaning all blood from his fist.

He came towards her.

"Hyy Mister, I am Bella Russo. He is lying. They are not punctual at all. My Oldest Brother Vinny always came late on breakfast, my youngest brother Ricc always goes school late and you just saw a example of my Middle brother, who told me that he is going to washroom and here he is chit chatting" Bella sighed dramatically.

Jason stifled his laugh.

Salvatore playfully glared at her and before she could run from there, he picked her up in his arms, tickling her.

"You little munchkin" He said swaying her from left to right.

She squealed and giggled.

To Be Continued...

Long chapter, ufff !

Don't forget to Vote and Comment on it.

Do you Like Salvatore ?

What do you think about Bella's Crazy and bitchy Mom ?

One Note to clear every confusion: Salvatore and Riccardo knows that Bella is their Niece not their Sister. But Bella doesn't. Not yet atleast. And Bella is Vincenzo and Shaira's (Their Aunt who raped Vincenzo) daughter.

I will upload next chapter soon till then stay safe, take care and Love Yourself.

Byee Byee... Luv ya.

Published : 15 July 2023.

Total Words : 2080 words.

Chapter 3

Author's P.O.V.

Bella yawned looking at the time.

She stretched her arms and a whin left her mouth as she looked at her Micky alarm clock.

5:22 am ?

She rubbed her eyes and opened her room door. She tiptoed to the beside room.

Without knocking, she entered in the room.

She came towards the bed tiptoeing.

She pout when she saw her brother is sleeping.

"Vinnyy" she said lowly.

No response.

"Vinnyyyy" She pouted.

Still no response.

"Vinnnnnnn" She whinned, annoyed that she is not getting reply.

Vincenzo opened his one eye and looked at Pouty Bella.

"Go sleep Bella" He mumbled.

"No, I am tired" She whinned.

"From what ?"

"From sleeping" She replied.

Vincenzo sighed. She yelped when she felt her legs suddenly rose from the ground.

Vincenzo picked her from ground and made her sleep beside him. He started patting her back trying to lull her to sleep.

"No Vinnyy, not sleepy" She yawned.

"Yeah I can see that" Vincenzo mumbled with closed eyes.

"But your eyes are close" Bella pouted.

"Hmm" Vincenzo Mumbled.

"Vinnyyyy" She whinned again.

"Hmm Hmm Bells" He mumbled pulling her close to his chest. He nuzzled his face in her neck.

She giggled feeling ticklish because of his slight subtle on his chin.

"Vinny it's tickles" She giggled trying to keep his head away from her neck with her small hands.

Vincenzo caught her both hands in his one hand and pulled her on himself and started massaging her scalp.

"Sleep Bells, it's still too early" Vincenzo mumbled with his morning husky deep voice. Bella felt his chest rumbled.

She pouted but get relaxed feeling Vincenzo's fingers in her hairs.

She started tracing her fingers on his tattoo that was on his chest.

Doing this, she didn't know when she felt in deep slumber.

Vincenzo kissed her head and covered themselves with blanket and slept hugging his treasure close to his heart.

In Morning... At 8:00 am

"Where are Vince and Bells ?" Riccardo asked.

"In their room, Ric" Salvatore said reading his newspaper.

"No Sal, I already checked Bells room. She was not there. I thought she will be with you" Riccardo said.

"Ohh then maybe we both know where she is, let's go" Salvatore winked and they both came infront of Vincenzo's room.

"You go first, I will follow you" Riccardo whispered.

"Why me ? You should go first" Salvatore argued.

"You are elder than me. It's your duty to protect me" Riccardo glared at him.

Salvatore scoffed.

"You are younger than me and I am ordering you to go inside first" He glared back.

"Shut up. I am not going in Lion's Den" Riccardo denied shaking his head.

Salvatore rolled his eyes.

"Drama Queen" He mumbled before entering in the room.

Riccardo followed him.

The sight infront of him melt their heart.

"Wow rabbit is trapped in Lion's paw" Riccardo mumbled.

"Shut up" Salvatore whispered.

He took out his phone and took a picture and smiled looking at it.

"Send me that" Riccardo told him.

Salvatore ignored him.

"Vince Get Up" Salvatore shook him.

Vincenzo squinted his eyes and frowned looking at his brothers.

"What are you both doing here ?" He groggily asked still one eye closed.

"Wow good morning to you too big brother" Riccardo rolled his eyes and go towards Bella.

"Shut up Ric" Both brothers said simultaneously.

Riccardo looked at them betrayed.

"Feeling so loved here" He said keeping his hand on his chest.

He lies beside Bella and pulled her towards him from Vincenzo who in response just glared at him.

Bella whinned a little but immediately Snuggled in Riccardo's chest feeling warm.

"Only My Babygirl loves me" Riccardo scoffed securing Bella in his arms.

Salvatore rolled his eyes and Vincenzo just stared at him blankly.

"Now shoo~" He said cuddling to his Baby, closing his eyes.

Salvatore shook his head at his younger brother's dramas. He signalled Vincenzo to come downstairs, who in response nodded.

Both elder brothers left the room after telling their younger to wake her up and come downstairs in 30 minutes.

Vincenzo get ready and came downstairs.

"Vince we have meeting in two hours with Mr. Astrod." Vincenzo frowned.

"Astrod ? Why ?" Vincenzo raised his one eyebrow at Salvatore.

"They are keep nagging to listen to their offers and deals" Salvatore rolled his eyes annoyed.

"Hmm. Ok then, I also wanna see what's special in their deals" Vincenzo replied coldly.

Salvatore nodded, continue reading his newspaper.

"Sal"

"Hmm ?"

"What happened to those Bastards ?" Vincenzo asked coldly.

"They are in lock ups, getting their punishment" Salvatore said blankly.

Vincenzo nodded.

Yesterday, when Salvatore told them about those Boys taking Bella's pictures, they were livid. Riccardo want to kill them. He even punched a wall making a hole. He so badly wants to hold their necks in his fingers. He so badly wanna feel their bodies in his hands.

While on other hand, Vincenzo was silent. His past memories started flooding in his mind. His past started crowding over his mind.

Why can't people let them live peacefully?

Why are they so disgusting ?

Why these disgusted people are making children their victim ?

Why are they ruining their innocence ?

Why can't they let children carefree ?

They ruin his innocence, his childhood but he will never let same happened to His Bella. He will give her a carefree childhood. He will protect her at any cost even if it means to hide from her that she is his daughter.

If hiding this from her, will save her from tormentors outside, he will do that willingly.

And at that time, he decided that he will make those bastards pay for their deeds.

Just looking at his Bella in a wrong way is a Sin in itself.

Those bastards have dared to take her photos, they will surely gonna beg for death.

And he will make sure of it...

To Be Continued...

Short chapter... Sorry .

What do you guys think about Vincenzo ?

About Salvatore ?

And about Riccardo ?

Don't forget to Vote and Comment Guysss pleaseeeee ...

I will meet you soon till then stay safe, take care and Love Yourself .

Byee Byee... Luv ya .

Published : 18 July 2023.

Total Words : 1038 words .

Chapter 4

"Ricc, you have a girlfriend too ?" Bella asked. Eyes focused on Titanic movie playing on screen.

Riccardo looked at her and chuckled.

"Nope Babes, I am Single"

"Why ?"

"Because, I already has one girl in my life"

Bella's head snapped towards Riccardo.

He is looking serious.

"Who ? I also wanna meet her" Bella told him holding his arms and looking at him with doe eyes.

Riccardo stared at her and laughed.

For him, she is definitely the cutest thing he ever see.

"You wanna see her ?" Riccardo asked looking Bella's eyes seriously.

Bella nodded.

"Wait" He said taking his phone from table.

"See. This is the girl in my life"

Bella's eyes widened.

"She is meee"

Riccardo chuckled.

He pulled her on his lap.

"Ofcourse it's you. You are the only girl in my life" He said kissing her whole face. She laughed feeling ticklish.

Salvatore came with a tired look on his face.

But the sight infront of him melt his heart. His tiredness flew away in a second hearing adorable giggles and laughs.

He took out his phone and clicked their picture.

He coughed gaining their attention.

Bella looked at him and smiled.

"SALLYYYY" She screamed, running towards Salvatore.

He chuckled opening his arms and she immediately jumped on him. He hold her in his embrace tightly.

"I miss you" She said kissing his cheek.

"I miss you too Princess" He said kissing her head.

"I miss you three, Sallyyyyyy" Riccardo mumbled teasing his brother, in response he just get glare from his elder brother. Riccardo laughed at that.

Salvatore shook his head and sat on the couch with her on his lap.

"Where is Vinny ?" She asked him.

"He will come later. He still has some work to do, Baby" Salvatore told her.

"Did you guys eat ?" He asked.

"No" Bella shook her head.

"Why ?" He looked towards Riccardo.

Riccardo sighed.

"We can't eat without Sally and Vinny" Riccardo mocked her.

Bella glared at him hugging Salvatore in process.

Salvatore chuckled at that.

"Bells you should eat"

"Noo" She pout.

"Yes I am hungry. Let's go and eat" Riccardo declared. He knows she is hungry too but don't wanna eat.

Earlier when he told her to eat dinner, she said she will wait for Vincenzo and Salvatore. So, to pass her time, Riccardo showed her a movie. But as it is late, he could see she is getting sleepy. He don't wants her to sleep empty stomach.

"But Vinny ?" She asked them.

"Don't worry about him Bells, he already ate" Salvatore reassured her.

She made 'O' shape from her mouth and then nod her head.

"Let's go" Riccardo cheered picking Bella on his shoulder, making her giggly and run towards dining table. Salvatore chuckled and goes towards his room.

Late Night...

Bella tiptoed to the living room.

Salvatore and Riccardo were already slept. But she can't.

She came towards sofa and sat on it.

She looked towards clock and then towards main door. She pout.

"Vinny when are you going to come ?"

She sat there waiting. Glancing at clock and door again and again.

But her ears perked up hearing tyre screeching sound. She heard a shoes sound and immediately ran towards the door.

Opening it, she jumped on the person.

That person stumbled a little, but catch her securely in his arms.

"You are late, Vinny" She mumbled holding his neck with her arms.

She heard a deep chuckle.

"Sorry Baby" He told her making her comfortable in his arms. He came inside the house and kept his bag on the couch, still holding her in his arms.

"Why didn't you sleep, hmm ?"

"Not sleepy" She mumbled snuggling more in Vincenzo's neck.

"Really ?" He asked removing his shoes. She hummed in response.

"Want to sleep ?" He asked her, locking the door behind him.

"Yeah" she mumbled.

"Wanna cuddle ?" He asked her, taking her towards his room, already knowing answer.

She nodded rubbing her eyes.

He chuckled and put her on the bed.

"Wait, I will come in 2 minutes" He said and goes in bathroom to get fresh.

He came outside in towel. He dry his hair, wore a pant and t-shirt.

All this time, Bella is sitting on the bed, sleepy.

Vincenzo chuckled seeing her like this. He goes towards the bed and pulled her to him.

She snuggled in his chest seeking warmth, wrapping her legs on his torso. He kissed her head.

"Sleep Baby" He whispered wrapping his arms around her, caressing her hair.

This is all she needed before falling in deep slumber. In a matter of seconds, she was out like a light.

Vincenzo chuckled.

Bella is always like this. She will always wait for them no matter how tired she was. It's like it is a unspoken duty of her. They always told her to sleep but she always refused. She will sit on couch and wait for them until they will back from the work.

And, They always come home on time knowing that their Bella is waiting for them.

When Riccardo was younger, he got involved in wrong crowd. He started staying outside of the house whole nights doing parties. Vincenzo and Salvatore tried their best to convince him. They even punished him. But he never listened to anyone. He was that Rebel kid. He just want to live his life. But unknown to him, he was destroying his own life. Drinking, smoking is ruining his life eventually. He never knows when he got addicted to it.

But Bella being Bella, a sweet 8 year old always waited for him on the doorstep. One day, He came stumbling on his own feet, drunk. Bella's eyes widened. She doesn't know why her brother can't stand by himself. She immediately ran towards him and hugged him. But, Riccardo being drunk, he pushed her. This broke her little heart. Her brothers never pushed her. They know very well how she loves physical affection.

Still, Bella never gave up on him.

And because of her love only, he realised his mistake on time before it gets too late...

And for this, he is always grateful to her. To His Bella. To His Babes.

To Be Continued...

How is it ?

I hope you like this chapter.

Don't forget to Vote and Comment.

 Your each comment just boost my motivation

I will meet you on next Saturday till then stay safe, take care and Love Yourself .

Byee Byee... Luv ya .

Published : 22 July 2023.

Total Words : 1092 words .

Chapter 5

"RICCARDO I AM WARNING YOU STOP DRINKING"

18 year old Riccardo rolled his eyes at his elder brother shoutings.

Salvatore sighed. Annoyed.

"RICC-"

"SHUT THE FUCK UP SALVATORE, YOU ARE ONLY TWO YEARS OLDER THAN ME, STOP LECTURING ME" Riccardo yelled and left the room.

Salvatore sighed.

"RICCARDO I DON'T WANT TO HEAR ANY COMPLAIN AGAINST YOU ANYMORE, CLEAR ?"

Hearing no response, Vincenzo looked at Riccardo only to see him rolling his eyes in attitude.

"RICCARDO RUSSO I SAID AM I CLEAR ?"

"Hmm" He hummed and left.

____

"Vince, he is getting bratty. We can't let him do all these things. We have to stop him" Salvatore told Vincenzo sighing.

Vincenzo rubbed his forehead tiredly.

"You are right"

That day when Riccardo returned after hanging out with his so called friends, Vincenzo grounded him.

And From that day, he started coming late at home.

Day by day, Vincenzo and Salvatore started punishing him. Sometimes they gave him homework, sometimes they gave him household works to do, sometimes they told him to babysit Bella, and whenever he started getting out of hands, they even spanked him.

As a result, he started rebelling more. He started getting drunk. He started smoking. He started partying late night. He even got arrested for some times. But, he felt like All these make him cool.

Vincenzo never wants his brother's life to get ruined.

But in all these no one noticed 7 year old Bella.

She always noticed how her brothers were always tensed. How her Favourite brother always comes home late and slept empty stomach. How there are always bruises on his face.

One day, after colouring her unicorn picture, she came out from her room.

But her eyes caught her youngest older brother.

Riccardo.

She ran towards him and hugged his legs.

Riccardo looked down immediately.

"What are you doing Bella ?" He asked her wearing his shoes.

"Where are you going Ric" She asked with her doe eyes on display. He stared at her for a second.

"None of your business. Go to sleep Bella, you have school tomorrow" He said blankly and left without looking back.

Bella frowned. She sat there on the sofa.

She kept looking at the clock then at the door. She started dozing off but still shake her head trying to pry the sleepiness from her eyes. She yawned rubbing her eyes.

Clock strikes 11:20.

She stood up from her place seeing Riccardo on a door. She immediately ran towards him.

"Ricc you are back" She said excitedly before hugging him.

Riccardo was not drunk that day. But he was clearly not in a mood to talk.

"Why are you up Bella ?" He asked removing his shoes.

"I was waiting for you, Ric" She replied innocently.

"Why ?" He asked removing his socks.

"Because, I was not sleepy" She told him.

He could clearly see she is sleepy. But still not going to accept it. Not in a mood to argue, he started walking towards his room.

Bella widened her eyes. She immediately started running behind Riccardo trying to match his pace with her small legs.

"Ric did you eat ?" She asked him running behind him.

"Hmm" He hummed, throwing car key in a stand.

"Ric you are going to sleep ?" She asked struggling with her steps.

"Hmm" He again hummed.

He came in his room and was going to lock it. But she entered in it.

"What do you need Bella ? Go to your room and sleep" He told her irritated.

"But Ric I am scared" She mumbled looking at him with doe eyes.

"Of what ?"

"Those white creatures" She replied.

"They are not here. Go and sleep. I am tired Bella" He told her annoyed.

"Can I cuddle with you ?" She asked pouting.

"Go to Vincenzo or Salvatore" He told her.

"They slept" She replied.

"Ughhh fuck it" He groaned, going towards his bathroom.

"Thank you Ric" Bella smiled ear to ear before climbing on his bed.

Riccardo came after some time and found that Bella is already sleeping on his bed.

He sighed and lay down on other side of the bed keeping some distance between them. He turned other Side, keeping his back towards her.

Actually he has a fight with his girlfriend. And he just can't concentrate on anything else except this matter. Because of this, Instead of partying right now, he came back soon.

Suddenly he felt a hand on his torso. He flinched but sighed instantly knowing Bella is here. He felt small legs on him.

He sighed and turned around.

He made her sleep away from him a little.

But Bella just kept coming closer to him. She is cold. She needs warmth. So, unknowingly in sleep, she is trying to cover her body with heat.

At last, getting tired Riccardo let her do whatever she wants.

And they slept cuddling and hugging together tightly.

Like this, days spent.

Riccardo started coming late again.

Salvatore and Vincenzo were trying their best to make him understand. They even locked him in his room but he always jumped from the balcony.

Bella always sat their on the couch waiting for him.

This becomes daily routine for Riccardo.

He even returned drunk, stumbling on his feet.

Bella's eyes widened when she saw her brother's condition first time.

She immediately ran towards him.

She hugged him but as usual he never hugs her back.

Why ? Because in his mind, his Bella is pure. He can't touch her with his dirty hands.

But in all these, he forgot how Bella always loves his hugs. How he is hurting her !

As usual Bella started sleeping with Riccardo in his room.

One day, Bella was dozing on the couch when suddenly she heard a door creak open. She looked at the figure entered in the house.

As usual, she ran to him and threw herself on him.

But this time, he pushed her.

Bella looked at him with doe eyes.

"Ricc" She mumbled.

His head snapped towards her. He glared at her.

He removed his shoes, and go towards his room. As usual, Bella followed him.

But like always, he didn't keep his door open for Bella to come.

"R-Ric I also wanna-"

"Bella, not today. Go to your room" He ordered her.

She pouted. Not understanding that her brother is not in the mood, she kept telling him to let her sleep with him.

Sighing, Riccardo said "Ok bring me a glass of water. I am very thirsty."

Bella's eyes sparkled. She frantically nodded and run towards the kitchen.

Riccardo closed his door and goes towards the bathroom.

Soon enough, Bella is back with a glass. She knocked on the door, but Riccardo didn't open. She pouted and knocked again. She frowned.

Why he is not opening it ? Isn't he thirsty ?

She thought before keeping the glass outside of his door and knocked on his door again with both hands.

But to her luck, Riccardo never opened it.

While, Inside Riccardo thought she will leave soon if he will not open the door.

But how wrong he was !

Poor Bella sat outside his door leaning on the wall.

"Ricc said he is very thirsty. I should keep it here." She mumbled keeping glass beside her.

"But why he is not opening the door ?" She pouted talking to herself.

"I guess, he is in washroom" She nodded at herself.

She kept waiting for him to open the door but it never happens. She eventually closed her eyes tiredly.

Riccardo yawned as he stretched his arms.

He put his sleepers and goes towards his bathroom to get fresh. After getting fresh, he opened his door to go towards kitchen but the sight infront of him made frown.

He frowned when he saw Bella sleeping there in water ?

When did she come ?

His eyes widened when last night events started playing in his mind.

"Shit- Don't tell me, she slept here, whole night ?" He mumbled in shock before picking her up in his arms. He felt her body is trembling. Her hands, legs, body is cold. She is cold.

As soon as he picked her up, she snuggled in his embrace mumbling something.

"R-Ric w-wat-ter-" He heard some words and he felt a pang of guilt in his heart.

In this condition also, she is thinking about him. And he ? He is so selfish.

He called Vincenzo immediately and told him about Bella's condition.

Salvatore scolded him for his carelessness and Vincenzo called doctor.

Slowly, she opened her eyes and Vincenzo hugged her, pulling her in his embrace.

"Ricc ?" She mumbled.

Riccardo's head snapped towards Bella. He never thought she will call him. Whole time he was just standing there looking down in shame and guilt.

"Y-Yes Bella ?" He rushed towards her.

"I am s-sorry Ric" She mumbled looking down. Riccardo frowned.

"Why are you saying sorry Baby ?" He gently asked her cuping her cheeks.

Her eyes watered.

"B-Because of me, you didn't get w-water y-yesterday-" She whispered.

Riccardo's eyes widened as his heart dropped. Never in million years, he thought that she will apologizing for something he did. It's not even her fault.

Riccardo pulled her on his lap and pushed her face in his chest.

"No Baby, I am sorry. It's not your fault. I am really sorry, Bella. Because of me, you were sleeping in c-cold. I am really s-sorry. Please forgive your b-brother" He sniffled hugging her close.

"Only on one condition" She told him seriously.

"What ?"

"Please Ric, don't come l-late from now. I felt sad when I saw how you got injury here-" she said pointing towards his face. "I felt sad when you can't w-walk properly, Ric, p-please-" She told him with teared eyes.

His heart melt. He stared at her. Her doe eyes. Her Pouty lips. Her puppy dog look. Her button nose. He gulped a lump in his throat.

Salvatore and Vincenzo looked at each other.

Riccardo nodded his head. He himself was not sure.

Bella's eyes sparkled and she immediately hugged him.

He chuckled and hugged her back.

"Ok Bella, go and get fresh" Salvatore told her. She nodded running towards her bathroom.

Riccardo sighed and was going to left the room when Vincenzo called him.

"Ric"

He turned back to look at his older brother.

"I know you are not sure. But just think about it, What would you do if she was in your place ? What if she also comes home late at night like you ? What if she also came home drunk like you ? What will you do if you also see her coming home every night bruised like you-"

"ENOUGH. I WILL NEVER LET HER" Riccardo gritted his teeth.

He could never in his life imagined this. He will never let her doing all these things. Never.

"So imagine how she must be feeling seeing you in that condition. You never know, but you are her role model. Always Remember that, Your Bella is looking upto you"

He kept hand on Riccardo's shoulder and said

"Always make sure to return home soon. Remember that, your sister is always waiting for you at the doorstep"

To Be Continued...

8 year Old Bella.

Do you like this chapter ? I mean small glimpse of past.

I hope you like it.

If you guys like it, then I will keep showing you guys small glimpses of their past like this... Through chapters.

More to come .

Don't forget to Vote and Comment.

I will meet you on next Saturday till then stay safe, take care and Love Yourself .

Byee Byee... Luv ya .

Published : 25 July 2023.

Total Words : 1960 words .

Chapter 6

"Why haven't you slept yet ?"

Bella flinched at sudden voice. She looked back only to see Vincenzo standing there, with his hands in his pocket, leaning on her door frame.

"Not sleepy" She shrugged smiling.

Vincenzo sighed and came towards her.

"What are you doing ?"

"Nothing much, I was not able to sleep so I thought of drawing ... Who knows, I may fall asleep !! By the way you are also awake, why haven't you slept yet ?" She asked him, continue sketching.

Vincenzo stiffened for a minor second before replying "Can't sleep either"

Bella's hand froze for a second.

She looked at Vincenzo and nodded.

She bits her lower lip knowing very well that Vincenzo has a nightmare that's why he is not sleepy.

But she didn't bring that topic.

"Vinny, can I ask you one thing ?" She asked him unsure.

Vincenzo frowned "Yes Bells, why are you even asking that ?"

Bella giggled.

"Can you tell me a story ?" She showed him her puppy eyes.

Vincenzo chuckled at that.

"Of course come"

They made themselves comfortable on the bed. Vincenzo covered themselves with duvet and dim their lights.

"Tell me which story you wanna hear ?" He asked her.

"Little girl's" She replied.

"Ok then listen, Once upon a time, there was a little girl named Rose. She was very pretty-"

"Like Ricc ?"

"Ricc is pretty ?" He asked amused.

"Yeah he is the prettiest among you three" Bella said.

Vincenzo rolled his eyes playfully "Why we three only ? What about you ?"

Bella looked at him in disbelief "What do you mean what about me ? I am The Prettiest one in this household. You guys can't even compete with me." She replied sassily earning a look of disbelief from Elder one.

"Wow, what a nice way to say 'You are ugly' !" Vincenzo exclaimed. She giggled.

"Ok ok we are getting out of track, Vinny. So where were we ? Oh ah- yeah She is pretty like Ricc ?"

He rolled his eyes.

"Yeah like Ricc" He replied earning a smile from Bella.

"She was living with her brothers-"

"Like me ?"

"Yeah just like you"

He said pinching her nose chuckling. She giggled.

"Her brothers loves her a lot-"

"Just like you all ?"

He chuckled "yeah just like us"

"She loves her brothers too- yeah just like you" He said before she could interrupt him making her laugh.

He started telling her a story and eventually found her breathing calm.

He looked down only to see her sleeping peacefully on his chest.

He chuckled, fixing her hair behind her ears. He leaned down and kissed her head.

"I will protect you till my last breath, baby" He mumbled.

"I am really sorry, Bella, that I am changing your school but I have no other choice, baby." He sighed closing his eyes.

Few weeks back, He got a letter saying Shaira- Their Aunt and Bella's biological Mother is back. And according to her, Bella is her daughter and she want her back. With her daughter, she want Bella's properties too.

She also sent them some pics of Bella.

When Vincenzo realised that She is taking pictures of Bella when she was in school, he decided it will be the best if he changes her school. So here it is, He changed her school.

If she can reach the school even after having so much security, then it will not take her even an iota of time to reach Bella. This alone thought scared Vincenzo.

What if she will try to reach Bella ?

What if she tries to manipulate her ?

What if she instigates bella against vincenzo ?

And what if Bella falls for her smooth talk ?

What if she doesn't believe in him like everyone else ?

What if she starts hating him too ?

Vincenzo will die. He is living only for his daughter, otherwise he would have killed himself 12 years ago.

But the thought of leaving his daughter alone in this cruel world, stopped his hand to kill himself.

Now if Bella leaves him, he will not be able to bear this shock.

He pulled her closer to himself and slept hugging her tightly.

Next Day ...

"Your school is going to start, Bella ? You want anything ?" Vincenzo asked her, while tapping keys on his laptop.

Bella frowned thinking something.

"Vinny, I want art supplies" She said, playing on his phone.

"Okay, then go with Ric for shopping, hmm ?" He told her.

"Yes" She beamed.

"Did someone call me ?" A very cheery Riccardo said in a sing-song manner.

Bella giggled and nodded while, Vincenzo sighed.

"We will go for shopping" Bella beamed.

"I don't think so you need shopping. All you wear is our hoodies, babygirl." Riccardo smirked teasing her.

She glared at him.

"I want art supplies" She stated.

"Why ? To make moustache on Sally's face huh ?" Riccardo reminded her of one of those prank, she pulled on Salvatore, when he was asleep.

Bella laughed at that.

"No this time, I want my art supplies to draw moustache on you" Bella replied cheekily.

Riccardo gasped dramatically.

"What ? You little munchkin" He said picking her giggly self from her waist and tickled her.

She giggled more.

Vincenzo smiled softly, seeing his little bean and his big bean laughing.

"Ok Enough Guys, Bella go and take a bath" Vincenzo said.

Bella frowned shaking her head.

"I did bathe yesterday only ?" She glared at him.

"So ?" Vince raised his eyebrow.

"So, now, I will bath day after tomorrow." Bella stated proudly, keeping her hands on her hips.

"And why tho ?" Vince asked amused.

"Because, My Miss told me to save water and save time. So, I am going to do both things together" Bella replied.

"Wow, I love this concept. I am proud of you, Babygirl" Riccardo said, impressed.

"Shut up Ric and Bella No-"

"Bella No- this is wrong habit, you should take bath regularly. Because Bathing is necessary as it cleanse our body. It protect us from getting any type of infection. Right ?" Bella mocked teasingly and continued with a little attitude "Yeah Yeah I know, I know, I was just kidding, Chill"

Vincenzo looked amused as she remembered his each and every word.

While Riccardo looked stunned as he gasped dramatically, again.

"You- You are talking too much" He muttered amazed and pulled her in headlock ruffling her hair.

"Leave me" She huffed.

She bit his arms and ran away from there.

Riccardo stared at her running figure, dumbfounded, before following her too.

Vincenzo shook his head, amused, continuing with his work.

Not even an hour later, His phone rang.

Without even looking at caller id, He picked it up.

"Hello" He said in his usual cold voice.

"Hellooo dearest Husband" His hands stopped in his tracks as his blood ran cold. He froze. His movements stopped. His mind stopped working hearing that voice. The voice which hunts him till today. The voice he hates, scratch that, the voice he despised. The voice which ruined his whole carefree childhood. Yes, Shaira. His Aunt.

"Voice get stuck in throat, hmm ?" Shaira mocked.

Vincenzo tightened his grip on the phone as his jaw clenched.

"How dare you to call me" He gritted his teeth.

He heard a laugh. Sinister laugh.

"Dare ? You haven't seen my dare yet, dear husband. You will see my courage only when your own daughter will fight with you for me."

Vincenzo's blood ran cold. His knuckles became white.

"I. Will. Fucking. Kill. You. Shaira. If you ever came in My daughter's life"
He gritted his teeth, standing up from his chair.

Shaira laughed.

"Your daughter ? I am her Mother, Vincenzo Russo. Remember, A daughter needs a Mom. For a Daughter, her Mother is her always priority" She smirked through phone.

Vincenzo chuckled, darkly.

"She is my girl, Shaira and I know her, she doesn't need you. She is my kid. I raised her. She doesn't need you in her life. So, come out from your fucking imagination" Vincenzo smirked darkly.

Shaira paused for a second before bringing smirk on her lips, again.

"Let the game begin, Vincenzo Russo"

To Be Continued...

Shaira Entered in the chat ... .

Share your thoughts about Shaira.

I know chapter is boring but wait more drama is on the way for you .

And Guyss...Go and Read Epiphany.It's a family and siblings story

Don't forget to Vote and Comment.

I will meet you soon till then stay safe, take care and Love Yourself .

Byee Byee... Luv ya .

Published : 27 July 2023.

Total Words : 1423 words .

Chapter 7

"Ric, it's enough" Bella scolded him, keeping her hand on her hips.

Riccardo showed her his tongue.

Bella gasped.

"You are kid" She rolled her eyes before rolling her eyes, and left from there sassily.

Riccardo looked stunned.

"Wow" He said and followed her.

"Let's buy-"

"No Ric, it's enough. Now let's buy something for Sally" She beamed.

"Ah no, old Sally has everything, let's buy something for Young Riccardo, how is it ?" He asked grinning.

Bella narrowed her eyes at him.

"My Sally is not an Old. You are Old, Mister" She scoffed.

"My Sally ? My ? Really ? And Me ? I am Old ? Excuse me, Miss, you are getting out of hands, I will sell you in teddy bear shop" Riccardo asked dramatically keeping his hands on his hips.

"Then, My Sally will buy me and then he will never give me to you" Bella smirked at Riccardo's smirking face.

"Heyyy, did you forget I am your favourite Brother ? Why did you keep calling that Old Sally yours ? You are mine and I am yours. Happy Ending" Riccardo huffed.

Bella shook her head.

"No, Ric, You are my favourite Brother but Sally is my boyfriend. And I of course love my boyfriend more" Bella grinned.

Riccardo's eyes widened.

"What the actual fuck ? When- how- what- when did all this happen ? Oh My God, that Old man took my girl away from me ? Heyy, you cheated on me-" Riccardo exaggerate.

"Nah Riccy, Sally is so handsome" Bella smiled dreamily. Riccardo narrowed his eyes.

"You Cheater-" He said snaking his hands around her waist, picking her up easily in one go, earning a fit of giggles from the girl. His favourite sound.

<<°>>~<<°>>

"Let's eat Pizza" Bella muttered.

"Okay. Wait here" Riccardo said and moved towards counter.

Bella sighed and sat on the nearby chair. She was tracing her fingers on the design pattern of the table cloth.

She was murmuring some songs to pass her time when her eyes caught something. Or someone.

Old Man.

She slightly frowned when she saw that man is actually staring at her.

She gulped and immediately averted her gaze towards Riccardo, who is just coming back with tray in his hand.

"Let's eat and then we will go for rest of the things, okay ?" Riccardo asked keeping tray on the table.

Bella bit her lips and again looked at the place where she saw that Old man but to her relief, there is none.

I guess, I am watching too many movies.

She chuckled at herself before turning towards Riccardo, who in response raised his eyebrow at her sudden chuckle.

"Why are you laughing suddenly ?"

"Huh ?" She looked at him surprised.

"I asked why are you laughing suddenly ?" He asked her, giving her Pizza.

"Oh- Nothing. I thought I saw someone staring at me there. But there is no one, I guess I am just being paranoid" She shrugged it off, before darting her eyes on the delicious Pizza infront of her.

"Oh" Riccardo said looking at the place where she point. He frowned looking everywhere but found none. Part of him wants him to believe that his Bella is just being paranoid while Part of him Knows that Bella can never be wrong. She literally has a great instinct. Her sixth sense is very powerful.

I have to talk to Vince about this.

Thinking this, he turned his attention towards Bella. She already started eating her pizza, moaning in delight.

"Oh My God, Paranoid ? Big word huh ?" He teased her, smirking.

Bella rolled her eyes "Of course, Not everyone is Dumbo here". She smirked back.

"Heyyy, you are literally giving me savage replies. That's not at all fair." Riccardo huffed.

"Deal with it, Baby" She teased him.

Riccardo's eyes widened.

"You Brat. This is all because of that Old hag. I will eat that man" Riccardo exclaimed.

Bella looked at him weirdly.

"First of all, He is Sally. My Sally. Not an Old hag. And I will not let you eat him. I will protect him" She replied.

Riccardo scoffed.

"God knows when all this happened. Just wait, Salvatore, till I get home then you can see what I will do with you."

He muttered.

Bella giggled silently knowing she made him angry.

You lose, Sally. I made him angry at you.

She thought before smirking cutely.

Flashback

"Nooooo Salllyyyy" Bella whinned.

Salvatore rolled his eyes and made her drink that bitter medicine.

"You are so bad" She huffed, before running towards tap and washed her mouth.

Salvatore chuckled at that.

That's her Vitamin B12 syrup. But Bella, of course never liked that Bitter medicine. She always gets angry with Salvatore after he forces her to drink syrup. But he always find it cute. This made her more angry.

How dare he not take her seriously ?

She came towards Salvatore and kept her hands on her hip and glared at him dangerously.

Well, for Salvatore, she is looking like a kitten. He raised his eyebrow.

"Salvatore Russo. You are very very very bad" She gritted her teeth.

Salvatore chuckled, and ruffled her hair.

"Heyyy Don't ignore me" She said in disbelief.

"Oh baby, I am not ignoring you" He smiled at her, fondly.

"I am NOT a baby" She narrowed her eyes.

"You are, baby" He smiled.

"I am Not" She narrowed her eyes more and commented with gritted teeth.

"Ok, you are big girl, baby" He said seriously like he was talking to a kid.

Bella for a second didn't catch what he was trying to say but not so soon after, she realised and immediately glared at him again.

"You are again calling me, baby" She point out.

Salvatore chuckled and shook his head.

This made her more angry.

"Heyyy you are laughing at me. I will tell this to Ricc and then he will punish you"

Salvatore raised his eyebrow at her.

"He won't, sweetheart."

"What if I made him angry at you" Bella smirked, cutely.

Salvatore looked at her amused. He kneel down infront of her, to match their height level and booped her nose.

"Did you forget little one that he is younger than me" He smirked.

Bella smirked back.

"Ok, be ready for the payback, Mr.Salvatore Russo" Bella looked at him proudly. Salvatore shook his head, amused.

 Flashback Ends

"Excuse me, Miss Sally's Bella" Bella flinched slightly seeing Riccardo's fingers infront of her eyes.

But she giggled at the name.

"Where were you lost ? I was calling you since last 3 minutes" He sighed.

"In Sally's dream. He is so handsome, right ?" She squealed.

Riccardo sighed. The fangirl in Bella is on full display.

"Yes yess he is too handsome. So handsome. Very handsome. Total handsome" He mocked. She laughed at his jealousy.

"Why are you so jealous huh ?" She narrowed her eyes.

"Because, he stole you from me" He pointed out.

"Not him. His handsome face actually." She corrected.

"I am the most handsome one, you know" He rolled his eyes.

"Nah ! Sally, then Vinny, and then you" She replied monotonously.

"Wowww" He looked at her in disbelief.

"I will sell you right now" He said and picked her up in his arms, making her squeal in surprise.

"They will make you sit beside teddy bears in the shop" He said nuzzling his face in her neck. She giggled loudly feeling ticklish.

They gained attention but who cares ? Not Russos atleast.

He came towards teddy shop with her in his arms.

Bella's eyes widened as she clunged tightly on him. He laughed heartily.

"Excuse me, Miss" He said politely.

Two women looked at him mesmerized by the handsome man infront of them.

He smirked seeing that shining look in their eyes.

"How much for this girl ?" He winked at them, silently signalling them to play along with him. Their confused face suddenly turned into smiley one as they nod their heads. Bella's mouth hang open.

She was just joking when she said Sally will buy her. I mean of course he will buy her but who is going to inform him that his Bella is sitting in teddy bear shop among teddies.

"But She is not a teddy bear" One of them said.

"Oh trust me she is. You know I will tell you how ?" Bella looked at him in utter disbelief.

"Teddy Bear is cute. She is cute too, see" He said and made her face to those women. She tried to pry his hands from her jaw and immediately hide her face in his neck, holding his neck tightly.

"No Sally, I am not cute" She mumbled on his shoulder.

"You can carry teddy everywhere. You can carry her too, see, I am already carrying her" He smirked. Those ladies cooed at Bella's cuteness.

Bella's eyes widened and she started getting out of his hold.

"You know the most important one. We can cuddle with teddy and we can cuddle with this girl too." Riccardo said, seriously.

"Ah- this is nice then" One of the woman said. Bella's eyes widened as she shook her head.

"Noooo I am not Teddy. Teddy never talks. I am talking, see" Bella ex-claimed in horror. Her mouth agape when she saw That woman extended her hand towards her.

She immediately clung more tightly on Riccardo. Her legs is on his waist. Her hands are around his neck and her face is in his crook of the neck.

"No, Ricc, Don't sell me, please, please" Riccardo laughed heartily seeing her and hold her close to his heart.

"I am kidding, baby" He laughed out loud with those two ladies.

"I hate you so much, Riccy, you know" She mumbled on his shoulder still not losing her hold.

"I am sorry, babygirl, you made me jealous so this is a little payback" He laughed. She bite his neck.

"Oww- leave me, it hurts" He winced slightly.

She pulled out and glared at him cutely.

"Did you know you just gave me hickey ?" He stared at her in disbelief. She scrunched her face in disgust.

"Eww. Yuck. I have to clean my teeth again" She said again holding him back.

He lightly smacked her head.

"Shut up"

She giggled.

"Ok, now tell me, what do you want ?" He asked her.

She looked in the shop, scanning through the room until her eyes stopped on the blue and white Teddy bear. Her eyes sparkled.

Riccardo followed her gaze.

"Give me that Blue Teddy" He told those ladies.

"Sure Sir"

They took that Teddy and left the shop after thanking those ladies.

"Ricc, I want to Pee" She said.

Riccardo looked here and there and took her near ladies washroom when he spotted one.

"Go ahead" He put her down and pat her bum.

She nodded, running towards the washroom. He wait there patiently until he got a call.

He looked at the washroom and picked up his call. He came near railings and answered his call.

Soon enough, Bella came out from the washroom after completing her business. She looked everywhere and found her brother, leaning on the railing. She started walking towards him.

But,

"Ah ouch" She mumbled pouting when she bumped with someone.

"Sorry, I didn't see you" She bowed without looking up.

That someone fake coughed gaining her attention. She looked up and immediately frowned.

A lady.

"You are definitely the pretty one" That lady said, smirking. She ruffled Bella's hair and left from there, smirking slightly.

Bella stood there stunned. She couldn't move.

A stranger calls her Pretty ? Strange.

Before she could think anything, Riccardo came towards her.

"Bells, what happened ?"

She looked at him and nodded.

"Your Sally called" He rolled his eyes.

Bella giggled seeing jealousy in Riccardo's voice, forgetting earlier incident.

Riccardo narrowed his eyes and again picked her up in his arms.

"You brat, laughing on me, huh ?" He said and kissed her cheeks multiple times. She giggled loudly feeling ticklish and they left the mall.

To Be Continued...

Mall With Riccardo .

Hope you like it .

Long Chapter guys, please fill it with comments and do votes.

What do you think about that Old man and then this lady ? Share your thoughts.

Don't forget to Vote and Comment.

I will meet you soon till then stay safe, take care and Love Yourself .

Byee Byee... Luv ya .

Published : 31 July 2023.

Total Words : 2066 words .

Chapter 8

"RICCARDO FUCKING RUSSO"

Bella giggled, keeping a hand on her mouth, trying to avoid any sound from her mouth.

She peaked her head a little from behind the sofa when she heard a heavy footsteps coming towards her. She immediately hide herself when she saw an angry looking Salvatore is coming downstairs.

"WHERE THE FUCK ARE YOU RICCARDO RUSSO ?" She giggled silently, again hiding herself.

"What- Oh Ok" Vincenzo came, hearing shouts from downstairs.

But soon widened his eyes seeing an angry as well as funny looking Salvatore.

"Stop laughing Vince, I am going to kill that shitass" Salvatore seethed while Vincenzo laughed out loud.

"Ugghhh Stop it, DAMN RICCARDO GET YOUR ASS HERE NOW" Salvatore screamed.

Salvatore's hairs are looking like a spikes. Like a cactus in the dessert.

Salvatore clenched his jaw when he saw that Riccardo did not turn up despite his many calls.

He looked towards maids standing there.

"Where is he ?" He asked them in cold voice.

"Sir we d-don't know" They replied, trying to control their laughter.

"Nancy" He raised his eyebrow.

Nancy gulped and pointed her finger towards somewhere.

Everyone followed her gaze.

Salvatore gritted his teeth and immediately marched towards the cupboard.

He opened the cupboard door and the sight infront of him made their laughter doubled.

Ricardo stood startled at that. Eyes widened like deer in the headlight.

"YOU BASTARD-"

Before Salvatore get his hands on him, Riccardo pushed him slightly and ran away from there.

"NO NO NO DON'T COME CLOSER-" He screamed running towards Vincenzo.

Salvatore's glare darkened. He followed him too.

"FUCK CLOSER, I WILL KILL YOU, JUST WAIT UNTIL I GET MY HANDS ON YOU-" He said coming infront of Vincenzo.

"NAH VINNY, PLEASE TELL HIM TO STAY AWAY FROM ME" Riccardo request, making Vincenzo his human shield and hide behind him.

Salvatore did not give up. His glare shifted to Vincenzo.

"Vince, you are not going to protect him from me today" He warned his elder brother.

Vincenzo raised his hands in surrender and stepped out from between making Salvatore smirk and Riccardo looked at him in disbelief.

Salvatore lunged at Riccardo like a lion lunged at his prey. But again, Riccardo managed to free himself from that lion's claws.

"YOU WILL PAY WHAT YOU DID WITH MY HAIR, YOU LITTLE SHIT" Salvatore screamed, following Riccardo around the House.

"BUT IT'S NOT MY FAULT, IT'S YOUR FAULT-" Riccardo screamed running towards the maids and hide behind Nancy.

"My fault ? Seriously ?" Salvatore growled, glaring at Riccardo and then stared at the maids.

They immediately got an idea and stepped out from between those men.

Riccardo gulped and again was going to run from there but this time, Salvatore hold his collar pulling him back, and grabbing him with his neck and put him in headlock.

"Where will you go now ?" Salvatore laughed evilly.

"LEAVE ME YOU OLD ASS MAN" Riccardo screamed trying to hit him but Salvatore is always two steps ahead of him.

"Oh yeah, now this old ass man will show his old ass power"

"NOO LEAVE ME ... What are you all laughing at ? Help me get rid of this cruel man." He screeched.

But all the people present there raised their hands on seeing Salvatore.

"No one will come in between" Salvatore ordered.

"STOP ORDERING THEM. AND YOU ALL I AM YOUR BOSS. LISTEN TO ME"

All of them turned towards Salvatore.

Vincenzo is the eldest no doubt, but Salvatore is the one who takes care of everyone in the house. No one can go against Salvatore, not even Vincenzo himself in house.

Seeing his glare, each and every maid scurried away from there.

"YOU BETRAYERS, I WILL PUNISH YOU ALL-"

"Ohh first take your punishment little brother" Salvatore smirked.

Riccardo gulped and started fighting him to lose his grip.

"Listen Sally, it's not my fault, it's your fault." Riccardo started.

"How ?"

"You took my Bella away" Riccardo pouted.

Salvatore frowned a little but soon widened his eyes when something clicked in his mind. He left Riccardo from his hold and Riccardo immediately took a step back away from Salvatore.

"See, I told you, it's your fault" Riccardo muttered setting his collar.

Salvatore glared at him.

"When did I get Bella ?"

"Not get ? No, You snatched her away from me"

"When did I snatched her from you ?"

"Snatched ? Bullshit. That's a small word. She has become your fan. She has started worshiping you. Now only your name remains on his tongue. Say anything to her, she will give you a reply with Salvatore only. My Sally is handsome. My Sally is not on old man. My Sally is my boyfriend. I will choose my Boyfriend over my brother. My Sally is the best. Sally this, Sally that. Fuck Sally" Riccardo groaned when he felt a hit in his head.

He glared at the Salvatore.

"What did you do that she became your 'girlfriend' ?"

"You fool. She made you jealous so that she could take revenge from me." Salvatore sighed.

Bella's eyes widened as she controlled her laugh.

Riccardo squinted his eyes.

"What does that means ?" Riccardo asked.

Guessing everything, Vincenzo shook his head in amusement but his eyes caught something as his amusement doubled.

He saw Bella's little head is peaking from behind the couch. He silently chuckled, when she tried to stop her giggles looking at the scene infront of her.

"I forced her to take medicine this morning and she told me that she would take revenge on me and see what she did to me" Salvatore sighed.

"Ohh" Riccardo's eyes widened in shock. Was she making him feel jealous all the time and nothing else, so that she could take revenge from Salvatore. This little girl-

"BELLA WHERE ARE YOU ?" Salvatore shouted, calling for her.

Bella's eyes widened. She immediately hide behind the couch, praying almost all deities to save her from these beasts. But to her luck, no one is going to save her from these beasts today.

She heard a laughing sound from the background.

"You guys are overreacting. My Bella is innocent. I don't think she would have done all this. I think you guys have had some misunderstanding." She grinned hearing Vinny's voice.

I knew my Vinny would save me.

She grinned thanking Vinny thousands time in her mind.

"I think you are right. Bella can't do that" She heard Riccardo's voice and squealed silently.

"Yeah Sal, leave it. Go and take a shower" She heard Vincenzo.

She could literally heard a sigh, followed by footsteps indicating that they all are gone.

A sigh of relief left from Bella's mouth as she slumped her shoulders down.

"Thank God ! If Sally and Ricky had got hold of me, I would have died today. Vinny saved me" She muttered, sighing.

"But, I got my revenge, Sally. I told you, I am born genius" She said and flipped her hair in attitude.

"It's time for punishment, Miss. Genius"

Bella screeched, immediately standing up away from the voice, keeping her hand on her chest.

For a second she felt as if her soul had left her body. She glared at the culprit.

Salvatore.

But her eyes widened when she saw all of her brothers are standing there, smirking at her.

They tricked her. Oh no.

She looked everyone and gulped.

Before she could think of running, Riccardo caught her in his arms.

"Uh oh Where are you running Miss Genius ? Now who is going to save you from me ? Your Sally ?" Riccardo mocked her and laughed out loud.

"NOOOO" She screeched loudly when she felt his long fingers against her ticklish spot.

"L-leave- me-" She couldn't even complete her sentence, when she felt another hands joined in her torture.

"So ? What you did with my hair ? Hmm ? I am not going to leave you today, you brat" Salvatore said, tickling her neck. She laughed out loud.

Giggles could be heard in whole mansion.

"Your boyfriend is Sally, huh ?" Riccardo said picking her up on his shoulders. She laughed now totally out of breath.

"Ricc will punish me huh ? Now I will punish you" He continued her torture.

"VINNYYYY H-HELP" She continued laughing. Tears started forming in her eyes due to so much laughing.

"Ok Ok Enough now. Give me My Bella" Vincenzo said pulling her towards him and rubbed her back trying to calm her down.

"Look what your Bella did to my hair" Salvatore whinned.

"You are looking handsome Sally" Bella said controlling her Laugh. Salvatore playfully glared at her and was going to lunged at her again.

She squealed and hold Vincenzo tightly in her defence. She giggled when Vincenzo also held her protectively in his arms.

"She is not wrong tho. You are looking handsome" Vincenzo stated, trying to fight the smile that is forming on his lips.

Salvatore glared at his Eldest Brother while Riccardo and Bella laughed out loud.

Bella stuck her tongue out at him and giggled when he was again going to get her but stopped by Vincenzo again.

The Russo Mansion is filled with laughter and giggles.

But it is said that happiness gets evil eye very quickly.

<<°>>~<<°>>

Bella sighed and pouted.

"Why can't I sleep ?" She whinned again turning towards another side.

"Tomorrow is my school and I am unable to sleep tonight. What if I can't get up early tomorrow? So I will be late on the first day itself. Oh God, no. I have to sleep. Ok Bella, calm down and just sleep" She gave herself a pep talk and again turn around to sleep.

Tomorrow is the first day.

What if I don't make new friends tomorrow ?

What if someone made fun of me tomorrow ?

Then, I will kick them just like Ricc taught me.

But then, Vinny will be sad.

And what if everyone made fun of me ?

I can't kick everybody on my first day itself.

"Agghh this is so frustrating. I wanna sleep" Bella whinned closing her ears trying to stop all those voices.

But to her dismay, her mind is not at all silent. She can't stop thinking about tomorrow.

She sat down on the bed and sighed.

"I don't think I can sleep today" She sighed and stood up from the bed, getting out from her room.

She tiptoed towards the stairs and came to the terrace.

Her eyes widened slightly when she saw someone already present there.

"Why are you awake, Bella ?"

A person said not even looking at her.

She was surprised.

"How did you know it was me and no one else ?" She asked startled.

The said person chuckled and extended her arms towards her. She grinned and immediately came in his arms.

"Because I can tell your presence with my mind in sleepy state too" Because you are my daughter. He thought in his mind.

"Vinny, you are the best"

Vincenzo chuckled and made her lay down beside him. She snuggled in his chest and looked towards the sky.

"So tell me, why are you awake ?" Vincenzo asked.

"I don't know. I tried but I can't sleep. I am scared, Vinny" She muttered.

"For what ?"

"Tomorrow is my first day, Vinny"

"So ?"

"So I am scared that what if I will be loner in school ? What if I can't make friends tomorrow ?" Bella pouted.

Vincenzo sighed, tightening his hold on her. He felt bad for her. He changed her school and because of that she is feeling anxious. He gulped a lump formed in his throat.

"Vinny"

"Hmm"

"You also went to school. Sally and Ricc too. How did you guys make friends ?" She wondered.

Vincenzo think something.

"By just being ourselves"

"Means ?"

"Means that We didn't change ourselves for anyone and people learnt how to love us for who we are."

"I didn't get it, Vinny" She pouted looking up at him with doe eyes.

Vincenzo chuckled and ruffled her hair a little.

"Always be yourself baby. Don't change for anyone. Always remember this thing that don't force yourself for anything or anyone. You are not here to impress anyone." He told her softly.

"But Vinny, I felt guilt that because of me they are feeling bad. I mean sometimes I felt like I don't want to do something but I felt bad by saying 'No' to them." Bella pouted, sharing her concern.

"That's because, you are soft and pure hearted girl, baby" He smiled, tucking a strand of her hair behind her ear.

"That's a bad thing ?" She asked confused.

He chuckled.

"No, sweetheart that's not a bad thing. But there are some bad people out there who is ready to hurt others. They will take advantage of your this habit. That's why, always speaks what's in your mind. Don't and I repeat don't let others force you to do something that you don't wanna do, hmm ?"

Bella think for something and nods her head.

"And don't feel bad after saying 'no' to the people because you are free to do whatever you feels like to do. No one has a right to force you. Always follow your guts and then you will see, you are going to be surrounded by the best people who will loves you the way you are." Vincenzo said softly caressing her hairs.

She listened attentively and nodded her head.

"I will keep this in mind Vinny. But what if someone being mean to me ?"

"Then like I said follow your guts"

"My guts will say to kick them like Ricc taught me"

"Then kick them" Vincenzo winked.

Her eyes twinkled.

"You are not going to be sad then ?" She asked curiously.

"Why would I be sad, little one ?" He looked amused.

"If I kick someone, the principal will call you and complain about me" She pouted.

He chuckled.

"You do whatever you want to do, Baby, your Vinny is sitting here, he will take care of everyone."

Bella's heart swelled with love and care. She felt blessed having Vincenzo with her side. She grinned showing her teeth.

She tightened her hold around his waist and snuggled in his bare chest, kissing his jaw.

"I love you so so so so much, Vinny"

Vincenzo as instinct pulled her closer to himself too. He kissed her head multiple times.

"I love you too, Angel" He whispered and stared at the sky full of stars. They sat in a comfortable silence staring at the beautiful night sky full of stars and a beautiful moon.

He sighed.

Because of stars there is no dark sky anymore. Just like, because of you, our lives are not dark anymore. I hope, I can protect you from everything and everyone in the world.

To Be Continued...

I am back !

Sorry for such a long wait... Now I will try my best to update regularly.

How are you all doing ?

Hope you guys like this chapter.

Bella is going to school .

Excited for the FURTHER JOURNEY ?

Don't forget to Vote and Comment.

I will meet you soon till then stay safe, take care and Love Yourself .

Byee Byee... Luv ya .

Published : 15 August 2023.

Total Words : 2528 words .

Chapter 9

"**I**f anyone bothers you then tell us, eat food on time, don't fight with anyone, focus on studies, stay away from boys, they are bad, listen to teachers, and if anyone makes you uncomfortable then go to teachers-"

"Just kick them on their shin, Babygirl"

"Stop it, Ric"

"You stop it, Sally, you are repeating this like 23rd time from morning, now please shut it off. My ears are bleeding hearing this continuously"

"Dramatic ass"

"You are dramatic, not me"

Salvatore rolled his eyes.

Bella, who is listening to them, giggled silently. Seeing them bickering to each other is always amusing to her.

It literally eased her nerves.

Today is her first day of school. She is nervous is just an understatement. She is scared. Nervous. Anxious. Tensed. And God knows what not.

"Bella, come here" She heard a voice.

Leaving her bickering brothers behind, she ran towards Vincenzo.

"Yes Vinny"

"Are you okay ?" He asked her, softly.

She sighed.

"I am okay but I am not. I mean I am healthy. But I am very nervous" She replied honestly.

Vincenzo chuckled and pulled her in his arms.

"You will be okay, my baby" He patted and kissed her head.

She absorbed in his warmth.

"Well, I have something for you" He whispered in her ears.

She frowned and looked up, still being in his arms.

"Wait" He said and extended his hand towards the drawer and pulled it and took out something like a box from the drawer.

"This" She frowned in confusion but her eyes widened instantly seeing what's there in box.

"New Phone ?" She gasped.

Her eyes widened. She was shocked. This is her first phone, of course she will be shocked. She remembers the first time she asked Vincenzo for a phone, and Vincenzo told her that she was too young for a phone. And he'll give her a phone on her 13th birthday. So, now so sudden, why ?

"But Vinny, this new phone ? Why ? I mean of course I am very happy but still ?" She frowned.

"I thought my baby would be happy to see the new phone and hug me with joy, but alas !" He exclaimed sadly. Faked.

Her eyes widened and she immediately clung on him and hugged his neck tightly.

"Sorry Vinny I didn't mean to hurt your heart. I really loved it. Thank you so so so much. I love you so much" She whispered kissing on his cheek again and again. He laughed heartily.

His Bella is really a Sweetheart.

"Chill Baby, I was just kidding" He chuckled, kissing her head.

"And I bought this phone because I realized that you are not a little girl anymore."

Bella's eyes twinkled "You mean I am Big girl now ? I am not a baby anymore ?" She exclaimed happily.

Vincenzo looked amused.

"Yes, now you are growing up. But yes, You are always going to be my baby, got it ?" He asked her playfully. She giggled and nodded.

Vincenzo again pulled her in his hug and kissed her head.

He's more nervous than Bella. It's not that Bella is going to school for the first time, yet he is nervous. He is scared that what if that bitch is again going to find her ? He can't afford that. Even though he said something else to Bella, only he knows how he has convinced his heart that nothing will happen to his Bella.

That's why he gave a New Phone to Bella. so that whenever she needs anything, she can contact him. He even increased the security around the school. Each and every corner of the school except washrooms and changing rooms has CCTV cameras now. He can't take risk at all.

<<°>>~<<°>>

"Take care, princess. Remember, I am only one call away, hmm ?" Vincenzo mumbled, kissing her forehead.

She giggled and kissed his cheek.

"Ok, I am going now, byee byee" She waved her hand and opened the car door.

He smiled and waved his hand back.

She got down from the car.

Running towards entrance, she turned around again only to see Vincenzo still there. She again waved her hand and saw him doing the same. She giggled and entered in the Eastway High School. One of the prestigious school. School for rich kids. Bella's previous school is also one of the best school.

The architecture of this school is even better than the previous school. The school's entrance is a study in architectural splendor. Tall wrought-iron gates, adorned with intricate scrollwork, provide a glimpse into the meticulously landscaped campus beyond.

Beyond the gates, a cobblestone pathway, polished by countless footsteps, leads to the imposing main building. The main building itself is a masterpiece of design, an elegant blend of neoclassical and gothic influences.

As she approach, she can't help but notice the meticulously maintained gardens that surround the school. One thing about Bella is that She loves Nature. And the fact that this school has manicured lawns, vibrant flower beds, and statues of notable alumni eased her somewhat increasing heart beats.

Walking inside, she came towards the cabin more precisely Principal's Cabin.

Approaching the cabin, she is immediately struck by its classical design. The cabin itself is a masterpiece of architecture. It boasts a timeless aesthetic, with its facade crafted from locally sourced stone, evoking a sense of permanence and stability. The entrance door, adorned with a polished brass knocker, exudes an air of formality.

Here goes nothing.

Thinking, she knocked on the door twice.

After hearing an audible 'Come in', she entered in the office.

As she step inside, she was immediately enveloped in the warmth of the past and the luxuries of the present. The interior features a symphony of wood, from the reclaimed hardwood floors that bear the marks of generations past, to the intricately carved wooden fixtures that harken back to a bygone era. Large, picture windows frame breathtaking views of the surrounding wilderness, inviting the outdoors in while filling the space with natural light. There kept a board with a 'Carlo Marino' engraved on it.

"Good Morning, Mr.Marino" She greeted politely. A middle aged man looked up from one of the file.

"Good Morning" He greeted with a small genuine smile.

"I am Bella Russo. It's my first day today." She said,

"Yes, I know, I already talked with Mr. Russo. Here is your Schedule for a day." He said extending his hand towards Bella.

Bella took her schedule from him "Thank You, Mr. Marino"

"Have a good day ahead, Miss Russo" He nod his head.

"Thanks Mr. Marino" She replied and came out from the cabin.

She looked at her schedule, going through all subjects.

"First lecture English" She muttered "D-216", looking here and there, she started looking for the class. She was moving forward looking everywhere but she did not find the class anywhere.

"Why is this school so big ?" She muttered tiredly.

"I can't find even a class, I don't even know what's I am going to do whole day !" She sighed, annoyed.

When she looked around, she saw a lot of students. The corridor is abuzz with the hum of conversation and laughter. Backpacks slung casually over shoulders, notebooks clutched in eager hands, they cluster in small groups, leaning against lockers and chatting animatedly. It's a microcosm of teenage life, where every emotion - from excitement to apprehension - is etched on their faces.

A faint smile formed on her lips. She don't know why but she felt good as well as happy that one day she will also stand in a group, gossiping and joking with her real bestfriends. The hope arose in her mind that the friends she had not met in her old school would be found in this school.

Shaking her head, she decided to take a help from one student.

"Excuse me" She called out softly to one of the girl, who is looking slightly older than her. The said girl turned around.

"Yes" That girl said politely.

"I am-" Bella cleared her throat "I am new here. I don't know where are my classes. Umm, can you please tell me where is D-216 ?" She requested politely.

"Oh yeah sure, give me a second" The said girl smiled and turned towards her friend.

"We will meet in class, See ya" She waved back to her friend and motioned Bella to follow her.

Feeling glad, Bella immediately followed her.

"Well hello, I am Alessia Conti. What's your name ?" That girl initiates a conversation before it turns an awkward moment and Bella couldn't be more grateful for that.

"I am Bella Russo" She said softly.

"Cool name. You are not looking more older, What's your age ?" She inquired taking a left turn.

"I am 12, soon to be 13" Bella replied.

"Aww you are young" She smiled.

No doubt, her smile is contagious, that Bella finds herself smiling.

"Thank you. What's your age ?" Bella asked following her.

"I am 15" Alessia replied.

Bella gasped "You are in third year ?"

"yeah, Third year of Scuola Secondaria di Primo Grado" She chuckled. (A/n : The "third year of Lower Secondary School" refers to the third year of education in the lower secondary level of the Italian education system. In

Italy, the lower secondary school is known as "Scuola Secondaria di Primo Grado" and typically covers students from ages 11 to 14 or 15.)

(I don't know if it's correct or not because I am not an Italian and I get this information from Chatgpt)

"And here is your class" Alessia smiled showing her a class.

Bella's eyes twinkled. She grinned.

"Thank you so much, Alessia" She said showing her toothy smile.

Alessia chuckled and went from there.

Bella waved her hand and turned towards her class.

She looked in the class with half door open. Some of the students are already present in the class. Some sit upright, notebooks open, pens poised, and textbooks at the ready while some are flipping through the pages of their textbooks. In the back row, a few students huddle together, discussing about something. While some are gossiping, laughing loudly. She could see no one is alone there. They all has friends. In all, Bella is nervous again. Her nerves which are eased earlier are now again aggravated.

She cleared her throat and entered in the class. Pushing open the door, she stepped timidly into the midst of animated conversations and laughter. Her eyes darted around the room, searching for an available desk amidst the sea of faces. Her arrival, unnoticed at first, brought a sudden hush to the chaos. All eyes instinctively turned toward her. She stood at the threshold for a brief moment, taking in the unfamiliar faces and surroundings.

She gulped a little feeling the attention on her.

As she ventured deeper into the room, the clatter of chairs and the shuffle of papers seemed to recede, as if the classroom itself were pausing to acknowledge her presence. Whispers and giggles dwindled into curious hushes as students turned their attention toward her, their expressions a mix of curiosity and speculation.

Bella finally found an empty desk. She settled into the chair, her gaze alternating between her notebook and the unfamiliar faces around her.

The classroom, once tumultuous, now bore the imprint of her arrival, a subtle shift in the atmosphere.

Soon, a middle aged woman enter in the chaos, gaining everyone's attention. Bella thanked all the deities at that time that everyone's eyes were finally removed from her.

"Good Morning Professoressa Greco" (means Professor or Teacher basically a female teacher).

"Good Morning, Students. Sit down." She greeted them back with a smile.

Everyone settled.

"I heard a new student came to class. Where is she ?" She said taking out a book from her bag. Bella bit her lips, again getting stares. She sighed. This is only a first day and she is already getting an attention. Twice.

"Come forward and give your introduction" Miss Greco called Bella.

Bella gulped and stood up from her place. Clatter of her chair is heard because of the silence in the class.

As Bella nervously approached the front of the classroom, the eyes of her classmates fell upon her with a mixture of curiosity, glares, judgemental gazes and warmth.

"Heyy, I am Bella Russo. I am a new student here. Hopefully we will all be friends." She said, nervously.

She could hear whispers around her. Some trying to smile at her way, while some just kept plain gaze.

"Bella, If you don't mind, can I ask you a question ?" One of the girl asked.

Bella gulped.

Does that happen too ? I thought in introductions, you only had to say your name and hobby. Is there also a question-answer session ?

Nonetheless, she nods her head, signaling the girl to proceed.

"Why did you join school midway ?" She asked curiously.

Some students display a calm focus, their eyes fixed on the front, Others exhibit an eager curiosity, leaning forward slightly in their seats.

Bella cleared her throat.

" I was in Alba del sole school, but because of not a good management there, My brother changed my school" She said softly, leaving all the important details.

Truth is, she herself doesn't know the proper reason of a school changing in such an emergency. But, she didn't care because she trusts her brothers blindly. She knows that if they asked her to change schools, there would be valid reason for her and she would never question it.

That girl nodded.

"Ok now, take your seat" Miss Greco said, turning towards the board.

Bella immediately came towards her place. She again settled into her chair.

<<°>>~<<°>>

"Can you tell me where is Cafeteria ?"

"Go straight, then turn right"

"Thank You"

"You're welcome"

Bella smiled, going towards the said path.

So far, her first day is going well. No bullies. No mean teachers. No fake friends. No abusive classmates. Everything is good.

As she walked through the bustling school corridor, her footsteps faltered when she caught sight of an unexpected commotion ahead. A cluster of students had formed a makeshift ring, their faces reflecting a mixture of excitement, shock, and concern.

She hesitated, her curiosity piqued, and edged closer to see what was happening. She slipped into the crowd among the people. Her eyes widened.

There, at the center of the gathering, were two figures locked in a heated altercation, more likely a tall angry boy is beating the another boy without any mercy.

Bella watched, her eyes wide with a mixture of fear and concern. She was frightened. In all her life, she had never seen someone so cruel. She felt like crying when she saw that injured boy on the ground. She wanted the other boy to stop hurting him, but she couldn't. She just froze in her place. She looked around only to find everyone standing there, cheering. No one was trying to intervene. Her eyes filled with tears. She swallowed hard as a lump formed in her throat. She couldn't bear to see someone die like this in front of her.

"Stop p-please" She said. but her voice was drowned out by the crowd. Her breathing quickened.

"Enough Teo" Another boy said calmly. And that said boy ceased his actions. They both turned towards the injured boy who is half dead now.

They glared at him.

One of them leaned in close to the injured boy and whispered something in his ear. They both smirked and walked away. Bella couldn't disbelieve it. How could be so heartless ? Eventually, the crowd began to disperse, leaving the injured guy alone on the ground.

Monsters.

To Be Continued.

Long chapter, guys !

I tried to write this chapter in a descriptive manner using Hard English words somewhat trying to write it in a Professional way. Please tell me, Is it okay ? Should I continue ?

I am thinking that now I will upload according to update Schedules i.e. Felicity on Saturday and Epiphany on Sunday. That way I can manage everything, so what says guys ?

Please show some love by showering comments and pressing that star icon below on left side lol.

Hope you guys like the chapter !

Don't forget to Vote and Comment.

I will meet you soon till then stay safe, take care and Love Yourself

Byee Byee... Luv ya .

Published : 26 August 2023.

Total Words : 2730 words .

Chapter 10

N ote : Above picture is : Salvatore and Bella (just imagine, she is 12 year old girl, not this short)

And, a preview for next chapter is given at the end of the chapter. Read it too. Enjoyyy

"-and then there was a girl. Her name was Alessia. She was really nice. She showed me the way to my classroom. She was senior actually. My classmates were not bad or mean. They were really good and welcoming. Well, actually all were good except two boys. Oh yeah, I forgot about them, Do you know what they did today ?"

"What ?"

"They literally beat a poor boy today in corridor" She gasped, remembering the incident.

Salvatore gasped too.

"You're shocked too, right ?"

"Hmm" Salvatore nodded, going to set the dishes on the dining table. Bella followed him.

"Trust me, I was shocked too and do you know what others are doing ?" She asked seriously.

"Umm, helping that boy ?" Salvatore said again going to kitchen to bring another vessels. Bella followed him again.

"No, I also thought that they will help him but you know they all were cheering for them" She said, scrunching her button nose.

Salvatore again come towards dining table to set those vessels.

"That's why those two were real big meanies. I felt so bad seeing that boy hurt" Bella muttered sadly, again following Salvatore from kitchen to Dining table.

"Oh"

"Yeah, then, after they all went, I helped that boy to the infirmary" She said.

"That's so considerate of you, babes" Salvatore said, kissing her head with a soft smile, again going inside the kitchen.

"Yeah, after that, I again-" She again followed him back to the kitchen.

As soon as Riccardo came downstairs, the aroma of freshly made dinner wafted through the air. He could hear the faint sounds of chatter coming from the kitchen. Salvatore was busy setting dining table while Bella was standing beside him, blabbering something. None of them noticed him.

"Heyy Sally, Heyy babyy" Riccardo said, picking her up from behind, making her squeal in surprise.

"Riccyy, I miss you" She said hugging his neck and snuggling in his embrace, kissing his cheek.

"I missed you too, Baby" Riccardo said, kissing her head.

He put her down and she settled herself in her chair.

"Sally, you didn't miss me ?" Riccardo pouted hugging Salvatore from back.

"Leave me, dumbass" Salvatore jerked his hand away. Bella giggled at that.

Ric gasped.

"You don't love me" He argued.

"Of course, Happy late realization" Sal smiled sarcastically.

"That's really mean, Sally" Ric put his hand on his chest, dramatically.

"Stop fucking calling me that" Salvatore glared at him.

"Why Sally ?" He pouted.

"Because, I don't love you ?"

"Why ?"

"Because, you are adopted" Salvatore smirked.

Smile disappeared from Riccardo's lips. He glared at him.

"Stop with that joke already" He rolled his eyes.

"Aww why ? offended ?"

Bella giggled. She loves their childish bickerings.

"Why did they start fighting again, Bella ? Did you do something again ?" A deep voice said from behind, startling Bella. She turned around and gasped.

"No, I didn't do anything, Vinny. These two always keep fighting." She said, offended that she was accused of something she didn't do.

"Point" Vincenzo chuckled.

She grinned, hugging him. He chuckled and hugged her back.

It was Bella's first day at school, so both Vincenzo and Salvatore worked from home today. Riccardo also wanted to stay, but the two brothers convinced him otherwise. Riccardo is currently interning to gain practical experience after his three-year bachelor's degree, and he's also studying for a master's degree. Even though they are wealthy, and Riccardo could easily secure a high-ranking position at B.R. Corporations if he wanted, he doesn't want that position handed to him easily; he wants to earn it through his hard work.

The aroma of a delicious home-cooked meal filled the air as they settled in their seats.

"So how was your day, Babes ?" Riccardo asked taking his food in his plate.

With a sparkle in her eyes, Bella was eager to share her experiences from her first day of school to Ricc. She had been looking forward to this moment all day, and her excitement was contagious.

Bella and Riccardo share a unique bond. While she shares everything with Riccardo, she also tells everything to Vincenzo and Salvatore. Yet, Riccardo is her crime partner, and she was eagerly waiting to tell him everything about her day.

Bella began to recount her adventures, her words flowing like a bubbling brook. She spoke of her new teacher, Miss Greco, who had a kind and welcoming demeanor. She described her classmates. She animatedly talked about her new friend, Alessia, who literally helps her on her first day.

As Bella continued to narrate her day, Vincenzo, Salvatore and Riccardo listened attentively, hanging onto her every word. They smiled and exchanged knowing glances, proud of the young lady she was becoming.

Vincenzo couldn't help but feel a mixture of nostalgia and excitement for his daughter as she embarked on this new chapter of her life.

Salvatore and Riccardo, chimed in with stories from their own school days, reminiscing about their childhood adventures.

"It was quite a sight, Bella, you should have seen how Riccardo was giving me puppy dog eyes at that moment," Salvatore said with hearty laughter. There was a smile on Vincenzo's face too, but Riccardo was only glaring at Sal.

"Why ? What happened ? And Ricc, you have puppy dog eyes, too ?" Bella inquired curiously. This just doubled Salvatore's laugh and even Vincenzo laughed at this.

"So, Bella, what could I do at that time ? I was left with no choice. I had forgotten to do my homework, and Miss was about to give me detention. I told her I had done it but forgot to bring the book. She said to bring one of my older brothers, so I went to get Salvatore. Like a normal human being, I told him to say that I did the homework in front of him last night. But this idiot wouldn't agree, so I had to resort to showing him those darned, umm shitty d-dog eyes out of desperation."

Riccardo grumbled, still glaring at Salvatore who is now red due to laughing hard.

"And you know what, Bella, after all that, do you know what Salvatore did ?" Vincenzo said, looking towards Bella with mischief in his eyes.

Bella immediately shook her head, curious to know what happened. She looked everyone with her big doe curious eyes.

Salvatore looked like he might pass out from laughing so hard, Vincenzo was also cracking smiles while Riccardo was just glaring at his older brothers.

"Sal literally came to Ric's teacher and said that Ric never does his homework, in fact, he never does homework himself; he gets it done by other kids. And if either of us scolds him for it, Ricc says that his teacher has told him that getting others to do your homework helps develop your leadership skills." Vincenzo laughed, remembering that incident.

"You know, Bella, I might have said that, but there was no need for Salvatore to tell Miss that. That old lady made my life miserable after that. She didn't let me breathe for a single day since then. 'Riccardo bring this from the staff room, Riccardo bring that from staff room, you wants to be a leader, right?' So do this, do that. Riccardo this, Riccardo that' Fuck Riccardo, I was so damn tired of listening to that old lady, and all of this happened because of this old hag." He complained shuddering at the thought.

"She literally haunts me in my sleep, you know" He grumbled.

Till now, all of them were laughing hard except Riccardo who just sighed. He looked at everyone and slowly a smile crept on his face. He just loves his Family so much. Seeing them laughing is kind of relief to him. He can do anything to put a smile on his family's face. And all that embarrassment is worth it for him if his family stays happy. He adores them.

He looked at Vincenzo. Vincenzo is his Eldest Brother but he loved him like a Father. When he should have been enjoying his youth, he took on the responsibility of three children. Despite facing setback after setback, he always kept a smile in front of his kids. It's not his right to give shelter to these two. They are his brothers, not sons right ? They are not his responsibility to take care of. He could have left with his daughter, but he didn't. He cares for them. He gave as much love to these two as he gave to Bella. He has sacrificed his happiness for everyone else's. He has fought the whole world alone but never let any harm come to his family. Riccardo worship his Eldest Brother. He could go any extent just to see a smile on his Brother's face.

His eyes moves towards the Princess as well as the Queen of the Family. Bella. By the way, in the family, Bella is his brother's daughter. She's his niece. But he has never loved Bella any less in comparison to Vincenzo. He was just 10 years old when Bella was born, and since then, he has considered Bella his own. He regards Bella as his daughter. In fact, Bella is his daughter; if necessary, he's even ready to adopt her from Vincenzo. Bella is his first child. Bella considers him her brother. He has fulfilled all the duties of a brother. They are each other's partners in crime. Together, they have fun, and Bella tells him everything.

And even today, he worries about her marriage. Can any random guy give her as much love as he and his brothers have given her ? Never. He has sworn that Bella won't get into a relationship until at least the age of 30.

His eyes stopped on the laughing guy. Salvatore. His second Elder brother. No matter how much Riccardo teases him, no one dares to say anything against Salvatore in front of him. He has seen when Vincenzo worked day and night to fill everyone's stomachs, Salvatore has fill everyone's plate even if he have to keep his empty. He can sleep hungry for a day, but he won't let anyone else sleep hungry. Salvatore has sacrificed his own comfort for their happiness. If Vincenzo is the pillar of the house, then Salvatore is the one who supports that pillar. He stays awake all night if anyone in the house is unwell. No matter how much Riccardo troubles him, he can't bear to see a single tear in Salvatore's eyes.

Nevertheless, it is the birthright and duty of the younger brother to trouble the elder brother. Today, Salvatore had a lot of fun; now it's Riccardo's turn.

"Well well well, Bella, do you know, our Sally here literally did a chicken dance infront of whole school"

<<°>>~<<°>>

"Bye, Bella. Ricc will come to pick you up today. Take care of yourself and eat your lunch on time. And if anything happens, just give me a call."

She nodded and kissed his cheek.

Salvatore chuckled and kissed her head.

"Byee Sally" She grinned, hoping down the car. He laughed and waved his hand.

After closing the door, she sprinted toward the entrance. Just as she was about to enter, she turned around, once again waving her hands with a beaming grin on her face. Salvatore chuckled and waved her back. With a grin of her own, she darted back inside.

She came inside with less nervousness than she had yesterday.

She was about to head towards her class but her moment was interrupted when she saw those two familiar faces from yesterday. Her smile faded.

There were those two boys, and one of them was once again holding a boy by his collar, while other boy is just standing beside them with his arms folded across his chest, totally unbothered.

Bella looked her surrounding.

Nobody cared enough to protect that poor boy from the clutches of those monsters. But Bella is not one of them. She is not a coward. Yesterday, She was scared that's why she was froze on her spot. But not today.

"You won't improve, will you ?" One of the boy whispered pushing poor boy in the locker more.

"S-Sorry-"

"I told you, hmm ?" He asked blankly.

"I-I-"

"Didn't I ?"

"S-Sorry-"

"ANSWER ME, FIRST" Poor boy flinched badly.

Bella, with her fiery determination, marched towards the scene. Her eyes blazed with a fierce resolve.

With a stern voice, she shouted, "HEY, STOP IT, RIGHT NOW"

Each and every head present there snapped their heads towards the source of the voice. Lots of gasps and whispers could be heard from surrounding.

The boys turned, momentarily taken aback by someone's audacity to stop them or to interfere in their work.

The crowd watched in stunned silence, as the tension hung heavy in the air. She could feel a heat raise up to her cheeks feeling all attention on her.

Those boys, leaving that poor boy stood infront of Bella with a slight frown on their faces.

No one dared to interfere in their work.

Who is this little girl ?

For the first time, Bella saw those two up close.

One, with his disheveled jet-black hair and a rebellious glint in his stormy gray eyes, exuded a rugged charm that was both captivating and intimidating. A hint of stubble adorned his chiseled jawline, adding to his rugged appeal.

While other, had chestnut hair that fell slightly over his brooding hazel eyes. His appearance was more understated compared to Jake, but there was a quiet intensity about him that was equally compelling. A subtle five-o'clock shadow hinted at his enigmatic persona.

She gulped slightly intimidating by their appearances.

"Who are you ?" Black hair boy said blankly.

She wet her lips out of nervousness and replied "That doesn't concern you."

He raised his eyebrow.

"Then this is our business which shouldn't concern you" Another one spatted.

Technically, they are right.

But Bella is not going to give them this satisfaction.

"Then stop bringing others in your business." She said pointing towards the boy who was getting bullied by them.

"And how do you know that he hasn't caused any trouble for us ?" Black haired guy said, folding his hands on his chest.

"Shut up. You are straightforward bullying him and you are asking me how do I know if he had caused any trouble to you guys or not ? Even if he had caused, you guys have no right to hurt others. Yesterday also, you guys were beating that poor boy. You guys are nothing but monsters" Bella ranted, totally forgetting her earlier nervousness.

Both of them stood there stunned. The crowd began to murmur. Some of them were plainly glaring at her, some are giving her pitiful gazes while some are just curious.

"Listen girl, mind your own business" Chestnut haired guy glared at her.

Bella glared at him back.

How dare he ?

"This is my business if you are going to hurt others" She gritted her teeth.

She doesn't know where this sudden ability to say all this came from, but she definitely knows she will definitely regret this later.

Both of the boys looked at each other.

Black haired guy sighed and said "Listen little girl, mind your own life and we will stay away from you"

In his simple sentence, there was an underlying threat that Bella immediately sensed.

"Or what huh ? What are you gonna do ? Bully me too ? Punch me too ? No, don't even think about that. I am Taekwondo black belted girl. Actually, I am warning you, stay away from students. If I ever see you hurting others, I will personally deal with you guys, got it ?" She said glaring at them.

When she didn't get any reply from both of them, she smirked.

Yess, She made them, speechless.

She mind did a little victory dance.

"Cowards" She left, flipping her hair from there with a small smile on her face.

To Be Continued...

Hope you guys like it ...

You guys didn't reply me in last chapter that are you all okay with weekly updates or not ??

Little Preview :

Xxx : Have you started your periods ? Have you ever had sex ?_______________

Yyy : Leaving bruises untreated doesn't make you strong.

Strength isn't just about physical toughness; it's also about taking care of yourself and knowing when to seek help._______________

Zzz : You ? Again ? YOU ARE AGAIN TRYING TO SNATCH MY GIRL AWAY FROM ME._______________

So, what do you think ? Who is Xxx ? Yyy ? and zzz ? according to you.

Don't forget to Vote and Comment.

I will meet you soon till then stay safe, take care and Love Yourself .

Byee Byee... Luv ya .

Published : 2 September 2023

Total Words : 2823 words .

Chapter 11

Classes went by in a blur with Bella not associating with other students and only trying to focus on her studies.

It was a free period and she was busy in doodling in her notebook.

"Heyy"

She looked up from her notebook.

"Hii"

The boy who was about to get a punch from those monsters.

"Mind if I will sit here ?" He asked her.

She shrugged her shoulders, giving him a little space to sit.

The boy took a seat next to her on the bench, and they fell into an awkward silence. Bella's introverted nature made it challenging for her to initiate conversation.

"I am Alberto. What's your name ?" He extended his hand for a shake.

"Bella. Bella Russo" She smiled shaking her hand.

"Well, Thanks for earlier. I was so scared but you literally saved me" He grinned.

"No, it's nothing. Vinny always says that we should always raise our voice against injustice. You know what, you should also stand up boldly in front of them." She said, confidently.

"Who is Vinny ?" He inquired, frowning.

"My Big brother" She said.

"Ohh. They are bully here. They both beat everyone here. No one has the courage to speak up in front of them. Everyone is afraid of them." He said, shuddering.

Bella gulped, a little scared.

I can always kick on their main point, right ? yeah of course.

"By the way, you are looking younger. What's your age ?" He asked, raising his eyebrow.

"Yes, I am 12"

"Oh"

"Hmm"

"Have you started your periods ? Have you ever had sex ?"

He asked, completely catching her off guard. Bella's eyes snapped towards him. Her eyes slightly widened. Her cheeks flushed crimson, and her heart raced. The abruptness of the question left her feeling utterly uncomfortable. She fumbled for a response, her mind racing to find a way to steer the conversation away from such a personal topic.

"Umm w-what ?" She stammered.

"I'm sorry, that was really insensitive of me to ask. I shouldn't have brought it up, yet." He apologized.

She slightly smiled, still uncomfortable.

"We will talk about something else" He said, smiling.

"Uh-oh sorry, I have to go now. See ya" She said, immediately sprinting towards the terrace.

As Bella made her way towards the terrace, her heart still racing from the awkward conversation with Alberto, she hoped to find a moment of solitude and respite. The terrace offered a tranquil escape, far removed from the crowded hallways and prying eyes.

She took a deep breath, inhaling the crisp air as she leaned against the terrace railing. She closed her eyes for a moment, trying to shake off the discomfort that still lingered from the conversation.

She couldn't help but replay Alberto's unexpected question in her mind. It had caught her so off guard, and she couldn't understand why he had asked such a personal question. As she gazed out over the schoolyard below, she pondered her feelings about the situation.

Bella knew that making new friends could sometimes be tricky, especially when people had different boundaries and comfort zones. But the abruptness of Alberto's question had shaken her.

But soon something caught her attention or should I say some'two' caught her attention.

There, sitting side by side on a far corner of the terrace, were the two bullies, who had tormented Alberto earlier. To her astonishment, they appeared anything but intimidating in this moment.

Their usual smirks and taunts were replaced by some other expressions. Their shoulders slumped, and it was clear that something had weighed heavily on their minds.

Bella frowned.

What they are doing ?

Bella hesitated for a moment, her curiosity piqued, and her instincts as a compassionate person led her closer to them.

She approached quietly, not wanting to intrude but unable to ignore the unexpected sight before her. As she drew nearer, she overheard their conversation, which was laced with something different than aggression.

"Is it hurting ?"

"Nah ! I am fine" Black haired boy chuckled.

Chestnut haired boy sighed.

"You really need to start taking care of these, Teo"

"It's fine, Mark" He smiled.

Bella frowned.

"No, it's not. It's not healthy to leave them untreated like this. You're getting too used to it." The boy named Mark- that chestnut haired guy said sternly.

The black haired guy named 'Teo' sighed, his eyes betraying the weight of his unspoken emotions.

"I know, Mark. But it's like a reminder, you know ? That I need to be stronger, better." He said, looking at nothing.

Mark sighed too.

"You know, you are already stronger, Teo"

"I know" Teo smiled. Both of them stared at the space.

Bella felt a pang of sadness wash over her as she listened to their conversation. She don't know why but she felt sad hearing them.

Bella, never change yourself for anyone.

Always follow your guts.

Remembering Vincenzo's words, she trusted her instincts and decided to
approach them.

With gentle determination, Bella came closer.

She cleared her throat gaining their attention. They looked up, surprised
by her presence.

"What do you want now ?" Mark asked blankly.

"Nothing" She rolled her eyes and looked at Teo's bruised knuckles.

She knelt down infront of them and was about to touch his hands. He
immediately jerked his hands away.

Bella glared at him and was again about to take his hand.

"The fuck you are doing ?" He stared at her blankly.

She sighed and took out something from her bag.

"Are you deaf or what ?" Mark narrowed his eyes.

"I asked you something what are you doing ?"

Bella took out a band-aid and a cream from her bag.

"I don't need those things" Teo rudely snapped.

"I am not even asking you" She mumbled opening tube's lid.

"Go away from here" Mark snapped.

"Shut up" She glared at them.

This made them stunned. First time in such a long time someone silenced them like this. They shared a glance with each other.

She was about to touch his hands but he again retreated it. But his moments halted when he received a glare from the younger girl.

Bella's determination was palpable as she approached him, her cute demeanor momentarily overshadowed by an unyielding resolve.

He glanced at Mark, who shrugged his shoulders.

Reluctantly, he gave in allowing her to treat his hands.

Well, it's not like she needs his permission but anyways, she gently rubbed a cream on his bruised knuckles, wincing slightly.

Both of them looked at her amusingly.

"You two," she began sternly, "if you keep hurting others, you're going to keep getting hurt too. It's a vicious cycle, you know."

She said, eyes still on his hands.

They glanced at each other.

"We never hurts anyone" Mark replied slowly.

"Yeah, and I am the Mafia Queen" She replied. They snorted.

"I am not joking here" She replied sternly.

"When-"

"Oh shut up. What will you ever get by bullying others ? Peace of mind ? Then, listen songs. Songs can calm your mind too, you know. If you want I can share my playlist with you. That's different thing, that I never listened any song from my playlist, my songs are always depends on my mood. Sometime, I will just listen only one song on repeat while sometime, I will get bored listening different songs too. It's sometime so complicated. Sally said, it happens. It is normal. So yeah, you can try music too. Bullying others is not an option. You can't go around hurting others. They are human beings too. They get hurt too. See, you hurt him- what was his name again- yeah Alberto, you hurt him and now you are hurt too, see. But don't worry, this cream will work. Sally told me to always kept this with me-" She stopped as she looked up.

Both of their eyes are wide opened. Mark slightly gulped too. While Teo looked stunned.

They shared a glances.

This girl doesn't have lungs.

She bits her lips, embarrassed. Second hand embarrassment.

"S-Sorry" She mumbled as her cheeks turned crimson red due to such embarassing situation.

She immediately took out a band-aid.

While wrapping it around his knuckles, she said softly "Leaving bruises untreated doesn't make you strong"

They froze.

What ?

"Strength isn't just about physical toughness; it's also about taking care of yourself and knowing when to seek help."

They listened to her intently.

"-and all done" She said, standing up.

"Take care and if I ever see you guys bullying or beating others, remember what I told you earlier, I will personally deal with you guys, got it ? Don't forget, I am black belt in Taekwondo, hmm ?" She smirked and turned around to leave from there.

"Wait" But a voice stopped her in her track.

"We never bullied anyone" Mark's voice heard.

She frowned but before she could ask anything. Teo said,

"And sometime, bruises are necessary. Underneath every bruise lies the power to heal and the courage to endure."

<<°>>~<<°>>

Bella sat cross-legged on her bed, her little mind consumed by the line Teo had shared with her,

'Underneath every bruise lies the power to heal and the courage to endure.'

The words hung in the air, heavy with meaning, as she grappled with their significance.

What's that supposed to mean ?

She scratched her hair a little.

According to Alberto, they are bullies. Infact she saw them bullying and beating students. Then why her heart is not ready to accept that ?

She clutched a pillow, her fingers digging into the fabric as she wrestled with her conflicting thoughts. Her heart yearned for the idea that there was goodness beneath the surface, that the world was more complex than it seemed.

Her eyebrows furrowed.

Why they said that they are not bullies ?

Did they literally lie on her face ?

Does they literally think she is a fool ?

She literally saw them beating-

"Oh God, stop thinking too much. Your little brain will explode someday"

She flinched when she heard a voice.

Salvatore come beside her.

It was an evening when Salvatore couldn't help but feel a bit concerned. She hadn't come downstairs after returning from school, which was unusual.

Deciding to check on her, he came to her room.

Softly pushing the door to her room open, he found her sitting at her desk, lost in thought. Her brow was furrowed, and she seemed entirely absorbed in whatever was running through her little mind.

He reached over and gave her a gentle hair tug. She whinned, smacking his hand.

He chuckled.

"What's got you in such deep thought today ?"

She sighed.

"No boys, right ?" He asked her playfully.

She rolled her eyes at that.

"Well, technically, yes" She replied with a grin. Her eyes dancing with a hint of mischief.

"Oh my God that's too early. You are too young for all these shits. You are not even a teenager, you are basically a toddler-"

"Sally, I am not a toddler" Bella gasped, offended.

He literally called her toddler ? A Toddler ? Seriously ?

"A toddler is a young child typically between the ages of 1 and 3 years old and I am 13, not 1 or 3." She glared at him.

"Well technically you are 12" He said with a sly grin.

"Still, I am NOT a toddler" She said in disbelief.

"Okay Okay, my big girl, now mind sharing what's going on in your little mind ?" He chuckled.

She sighed and leaned towards his chest. He picked her up from her desk and made themselves comfortable on the bed. She hugged him. Her head on his chest, legs on his legs and hands on his stomach. Totally comfortable. While, his hands are caressing her hair, relaxing her scalp.

They sat in silence.

"Sally"

"Hmm"

"Can I ask you one thing ?"

"No"

"Ok. What do you think what this means 'Underneath every bruise lies the power to heal and the courage to endure' ?"

Salvatore frowned. He knew that something is definitely bothering her but this was unexpected. He was expecting like 'why some boys are always doing show off, why some girls are always like to be mean, why some couples are so cringey' but bruises ? He never expected that.

Nonetheless, he thinks something and said,

"You know, when we face difficult or painful experiences, there is an innate capacity within us to heal and find the courage to persevere."

"That's too hard" She scrunched her nose. He chuckled.

"That means that when life gets tough or we go through painful times, we have a natural ability inside us to recover and keep going, even if it's hard. It's like having an inner strength that helps us get through tough situations."

"Ooh" She nodded, now getting it.

"Just as a bruise eventually fades and the body's natural healing processes kick in, so too can we overcome emotional or physical wounds." He continued "That's why some bruises are kept unhealed so that it could heal naturally and shows us that there is something inside us, which can heal us with time, naturally" He said with a distant look in his eyes.

Bella looked up.

"That means We shouldn't treat bruises ?" She tilted her head in confusion.

Salvatore snapped out from his thoughts. He chuckled.

That's why he called her 'little brain'

"Nope, princess, bruises should be treated because Bruises may toughen the skin, but they don't heal the soul." He said with smile.

Her eyes twinkled.

"Then, I did right thing." She beamed.

He frowned.

"What ?"

"You know what happened today-" and there she told him everything about the day.

He stiffened when she told him about Alberto asking her for periods and sex. He even asked her if he said or asked or touched her anywhere but she shook her head, giving him a relief. He took a mental note to inform this to his brother later.

"I am thinking about them. Mark and Teo. They said that they are not bullies but Alberto said they are. Even I saw them beating students" She mumbled.

Salvatore heard her. Call it brotherly instinct, but he could tell that Alberto is not someone he should believe on. But, he also don't know other two kids too.

He caressed her hair.

"Bells, you know sometimes what you see is not necessarily what it is."

"Means ?" She furrowed her eyebrows.

"Means what you see with your eyes can also be wrong." He said, flicking her forehead lightly.

"There could be a more story to it too that you are not aware of, hmm ?"

"Oh" She said.

He is right. She shouldn't judge anyone that easily.

His words are roaming around in her little brain.

"Now stop this. I can literally see your brain is tired of thinking these shits" He said, again flicking her forehead. She groaned and rubbed it.

"And stop talking about other boys, I am feeling jealous" He pouted, playfully.

She giggled at that.

But their sweet moment get interrupted by a loud thud.

"You ? Again ? YOU ARE AGAIN TRYING TO SNATCH MY GIRL AWAY FROM ME"

"Shut up, Ricc" Sal rolled his eyes.

"Whatever. Bells, let's go and watch movie" Riccardo grinned, practically snatching her from Salvatore's hold, who in response cursed him.

He didn't pay attention to it and ran away from there.

"Oh God, I was waiting for you from such a long time" Vincenzo exclaimed when they entered in home theatre.

"VINNYYY" She squealed and jumped in his arms.

"My baby" He said kissing her cheek.

He had gone since morning for some projects even before she went to school. So, yeah she missed him.

"If your drama is over, Can I take my girl now ?" Riccardo asked plainly.

"Nope, you can take your boy" Vincenzo said, pointing towards the door, where Salvatore just entered.

Riccardo scrunched his nose.

"That's disgusting"

"You are disgusting" Salvatore's voice heard.

"Oh, yeah, because I am related to you ?" Ricc mocked.

"That's why you are still here, alive"

"Oh well-"

Vincenzo sighed, while Bella giggled.

Salvatore - Riccardo and their never ending bickerings !!!!

To Be Continued...

Hope you like this chapter... .

What do you think about Alberto ? Why he asked her about those things ? Who is telling truth ? Mark/Teo or Alberto ? Share your thoughts about the chapter .

It's 3:00 am here . I am tired now. I am going to sleep now . Good Night . Sweet Dreams . Take care . (Edited : This was a time when I wrote this chapter.)

Little Preview:

Xxx : Oh God, which princess is not bathing, babes ?_______________

Yyy : If it means everyone will give me a hug, does that mean even Mommy will hug me ?_______________

Zzz : AND DON'T GIVE MY BABIES TO THAT MONSTER NAMED RIC. HE WILL EAT THEM IN DINNER._______________

Xyz : Because you are Poopy princess._______________

Guess Xxx, yyy, zzz, and Xyz.

Don't forget to Vote and Comment.

I will meet you soon till then stay safe, take care and Love Yourself .

Byee Byee... Luv ya .

Published : 7 September 2023.

Total Words : 2842 words .

Chapter 12

Vincenzo : 18 Years OldSalvatore : 16 Years OldRiccardo : 14 Years OldBella : 4 Years Old

"BELLA, BELLA"

A loud voice reverberated through the corridor, followed by a chorus of adorable giggles.

"BELLA STOP HIDING AND COME OUT AT THIS INSTANT"

She giggled and shook her head, knowing very well that he can't see her.

"Bella, I am warning you, if you are not going to come out at this instant, I will give all your dolls and princess to Ric"

Bella gasped at the threat.

These aren't just princesses and dolls, They're her kids, and she is their mommy. She raised them. Why is the world being so mean, trying to take them away from her ? And giving them to a scary monster who might eat them for dinner ? Oh no, she can't let that meanie named Ric eat her babies for dinner.

"Gotcha !"

Bella flinched ever so slightly, caught off guard by her brother's unexpected arrival, her little heart racing for a moment. Her wide eyes blinked in surprise.

Vincenzo chuckled as he saw the look of surprise on Bella's face.

"It's time for your bath, little explorer."

Bella's eyes widened once more as she attempted to crawl away from her inquisitive brother, but he deftly caught her little feet before she could unleash more of her playful stunts.

"No No No ... You can't hide more, now, come on, let's give you a bath" He said pulling her towards him.

"Noooooo, Bella need baby" She whinned.

"Bella's Babies are here only. She can have them after taking a bath" Vincenzo said and picked her whinning self.

"But Vinnyyy, Bella no like bath" She mumbled, pouting.

"Then what does Bella like ?" He asked as he kissed her cheeks and took her to her attached bathroom.

Her eyes sparkled.

"Bella likes babies, food- nuh uh not that yucky gross food but ice-ceam, waffy, cake, cholate and oh yes, Bella like fozen, Elsa, Anna, sow white, cindella, Aiel, Belle- you know Vinny, Belle is my favoite" She told him.

He made her sit on a toilet seat.

"Why ?"

"Becuz, we both have same names. I am Bella. She is Belle." Bella said with a most beautiful smile on her face. She felt proud of herself.

Vincenzo nodded, encouraging her to share more. "That's really amazing, Bells"

"You know, Vinny, She's got the most beautiful golden hair and the pettiest yellow dwess. She loves books, just like me, Vinny ! And she's so kind and brave."

"Oh just like you, princess"

"Yes yes yes, Vinny" She chirped, grinning.

"Oh, What adventures do you think Belle is going on today ?" Vincenzo asked, keeping her busy in conversation as he started preparing her bathing tub.

Bella's imagination soared as she narrated an enchanting tale of Belle's adventures, involving talking teacups, dancing candlesticks, and, of course, the Beast.

"You know Vinny, Beast was kinda scawy at fiwst, but then he's nice."

As she spoke, Vincenzo quietly gathered her bath supplies - a fluffy towel, a rubber duck, soap, and her cozy pajamas with a Belle picture.

He made her stand and removed her clothes.

"Now, Belle is having a magical dance with the Beast in the grand ball-woom" She said, grinning.

Vincenzo grinned.

"Yes, and now you come here, It's time for you to have your own magical adventure in the bathtub!"

Bella's eyes widened as she looked down.

Her mouth agape. Her Vinny tricked her ?

She gasped.

He turned around to put her clothes in the laundry basket when a thought suddenly clicked in Bella's mind, causing her to bolt away from the bathroom.

"Now, my little Bella will enjoy her bathing with her royal guest princess Belle and then-"

But when he turned back, he was met with an empty bathroom.

A mischievous grin spread across Bella's face as she seized this golden opportunity to evade bath time. Her tiny feet pattered against the tiled floor as she scampered away, her laughter echoing through the hallway.

Vincenzo sighed tiredly, knowing exactly what had happened. He called out, "BELLA, COME BACK"

He came out from her bathroom.

"BELLA"

But there was no response except for more giggles.

He followed Bella's peals of laughter as she darted through the living room, her little body a streak of movement.

"Heyy, don't run, baby, you need a bath, come back to me" He tried to coax her but she just shook her head running away.

Their chase continued around the living room, with Bella's laughter and Vincenzo's gentle admonitions filling the air.

"Bella, I will really give your princess and dolls to Ric" He threatened her.

"NOOOO Vinnnyyyy pleaseeee. They are Bella's babiesss" She whinned still running away from him.

But how far could her little legs take her ? Her tiny steps couldn't keep up with Vincenzo's long strides !

"Gotcha!" he exclaimed as he playfully scooped her up into his arms, her tiny body wriggling with glee. Bella laughed and squirmed, attempting to escape her impending bath.

"Nooo vinnyy leave meee" She struggled.

"No princess, you should take a bath"

"No, princess don't bathe" She screeched.

Vincenzo couldn't help but chuckle at her creativity and determination. He knew that Bella had a vivid imagination and loved to role-play as a princess.

However, bath time was non-negotiable.

With a patient smile, he said, "Even princesses need to stay clean, my little royal. It's time for your bath."

"Nooooo" She yelled, her tiny legs kicking in air trying to free herself from her eldest brother's iron grip.

"Oh God, which princess is not bathing, babes ?" Salvatore laughed, listening to Bella's excuses of not bathing, as he entered in the living room.

Her eyebrows furrowed.

"Every princess Sally" She said with a determination.

"Oh baby" He shook his head.

"You are so cutee" He gushed kissing her head, cheeks, eyes, her whole face.

"Princess are always cute, Sally. I am also princess. So, I am cute" She grinned.

Salvatore laughed.

"She is really a sassy queen, huh ?"

Vincenzo grinned and nodded "Of course, she is my sassy queen, right baby ?" He said repeatedly kissing her cheeks, making her giggle silently.

He bought her in bathroom again and made her sit in a tub.

"Vinny, no bath, please"

"No princess, you have to"

He said and the bubbly water greeted her tiny body with warmth, enveloping her in a cocoon of comfort.

"Dada, I no like bath" She whispered slowly this time.

Vincenzo's hands stopped as he looked at her. Pouty lips with teary eyes. His heart broke.

He sighed.

"I know baby, I know" His voice was painful.

He cupped her little face and said in his softest voice "Baby, you trust Vinny, right ?"

She immediately nodded her head.

"Then, relax. You know bathing is very important. The warm water can wash away any dirt and make your skin soft and smooth. After a bath, you'll smell so nice that everyone will want to give you a big hug ! But don't worry, I am not going to give you to anyone" Vincenzo said softly.

Bella listened to him intently.

"If it means everyone will give me a hug, does that mean even Mommy will hug me ?" She said with stars in her eyes.

Vincenzo's hands stopped in mid.

His heart broke for a little girl. She is craving for a Mother, Mother's love, Mother's warmth, Mother's care. But-

He sighed, controlling himself and smiled at her.

Vincenzo's gentle hands started his work.

"Bella, everyone even your princess Belle will hug you"

Her eyes widened.

"Really ?"

He smiled and nodded.

He lathered the baby soap, Bella's little fingers couldn't resist making soap bubbles that floated around her like tiny, glistening jewels.

"Bathing makes you feel fresh and clean, like a superhero ready for action ! It's like a magical water adventure, and you get to be the captain of your ship ! You can have fun splashing in the water and playing with your favorite bath toys during bathing you know"

She immediately giggled as she splashed water.

"Yes, just like that and you know what is more interesting ?" He asked.

With a careful rinse and the swish of the final rinse cup, bath time neared its end.

"What ?" She asked, her doe eyes are looking very curious.

Her playful splashes turned into gentle kicks as she soaked up the joy of the bath, her bath toys floating beside her.

"Bathing helps you sleep better, so you'll have sweet dreams of your favourite Princess Belle and after you're all clean, we can snuggle up with a cozy blanket and your favorite bedtime story." He grinned.

"And if anyone will disturb us, we will give them to the tickle monsters" He told her, tickling her side.

Her laughter filled the bathroom.

He gently lifted her from the tub, wrapping her in a warm towel, cocooning her in its softness. She nestled into the towel with a contented sigh, feeling snug and loved.

With a smile, he made her wear her clothes, dried her hair with a towel and combed it making a little braid.

"Now you can play with your babies" He said, setting her down on her feet.

She immediately run towards her dolls and princesses.

Vincenzo chuckled and was about to leave the room when he heard "AND DON'T GIVE MY BABIES TO THAT MONSTER NAMED RIC. HE WILL EAT THEM IN DINNER"

Vincenzo laughed at that and shook his head.

That's who Bella is. His little daughter.

<<°>>~<<°>>

"VINNY"

Vincenzo looked up from his books.

"What happened, Bells ? Why are you crying ?" He frowned, seeing her.

"Vinny, I poop" She pouted.

Riccardo laughed at that. Salvatore smacked his head.

Vincenzo sighed, shaking his head with a smile.

"Ok wait, Ric, go and clean her-"

"What ? Me ?" Riccardo asked, shocked.

"Nope, your ghost, of course you idiot, go and clean her" Salvatore rolled his eyes.

"Vincee, nooo, Why don't you tell Sally to do this ?" He pouted.

"Stop calling me, Sally, idiot" Salvatore glared at him.

"Sal, don't call your brother 'Idiot' and Ric, Sal is making dinner, right ?" Vincenzo said softly.

"Yes, if you are going to make dinner then I will clean her" Salvatore said, knowing very well that no one except him knows how to cook.

Bella sat there on the floor, with criss-crossed leg, watching her brothers interacting with each other.

Riccardo turned towards Vincenzo.

"Why don't you do this ?" He pouted.

Vincenzo shrugged his shoulders "Alright, I'll clean her up, you go and tidy her room thoroughly, okay ?"

Riccardo's eyes immediately widened. He doesn't like to clean her room. God knows what's going on in his head. It's not like, he is going to find any condom or bra there.

"No No, I am going" He stood up and immediately picked Bella up in his arms, and ran towards the washroom.

Vincenzo and Salvatore chuckled at that.

Their little brother can be quite a handful at times.

With a grumble, Ric reluctantly entered the bathroom.

He made her stand there.

Ric let out a sigh of resignation as he began the process. First, he gingerly removed Bella's soiled diaper, making sure to minimize any further mess. He muttered to himself "Why do she poop so much ?"

Bella, on the other hand, giggled at Ric's annoyance. "Silly Riccy," she chimed in, "I don't know !"

"But, I know" He smirked, thinking something.

He wiped her clean with baby wipes.

"Why ?" Her eyebrows furrowed.

"Because you are Poopy princess" He grinned.

"Yess, I am princess" She grinned too.

He chuckled "Not only princess, but a poopy princess"

"Poopy ?"

Her eyes filled with confusion.

She never heard about poopy princess. She knows Elsa, Anna, Mulan, Snow white, Cinderella, Rapunzel, Belle and many more but poopy princess ? No, she never heard about it. Is she new in princess world ?

Riccardo, still wiping away the mess, replied,

"Yes, Poopy" He grinned, seeing her thinking very hard about this.

Bella's eyes twinkled with excitement.

"Really ? I am poopy princess ?" She beamed.

He bit his lips to control his laughing.

Ric's grumbling began to subside as he indulged his sister in a chat about her being the poopy princess.

"Yeah ofcourse, from the date you're born, I am calling you Poopy princess but Vinny and Sally scold me" Riccardo pouted. But this time it was fake.

"Yess, I am poopy princess" She squealed.

He laughed hard.

After finishing the cleaning process, he helped her put on a fresh diaper.

"So, what are you, My Bella ?"

"A poopy princess" She cheered, grinning ear to ear.

He washed his hands and helped Bella wash hers.

"Again, repeat, what are you ?"

"POOPY PRINCESS" She cheered loudly.

He laughed out loud.

"Yes, a Poopy princess"

"Poopy princess" She repeats with a wide grin.

"Yess, now go and tell this to Sally and Vinny, go go" He said and patted her bum to go.

She immediately ran towards her other brothers.

"VINNYYY, SALLYYY, I AM POOPY PRINCESS"

To Be Continued...

Like this chapter ? Yes or no ?

4 year old Bella is crazyyyy but cute , isn't she ?

Share your thoughts about this chapter.

Little Preview :

Xxx : You are very cute. Be my girlfriend._________________

Yyy : I guess I am watching things. For a second, I thought I saw someone there staring at us._________________

Zzz : I saw her today. She is looking so happy with them, I guess.

Xyz : oh, not for long. It's time to call him. *Smirk*

I will come in your life, soon *Laugh loudly*_____________________

So, here is preview, guess what's going to happen in next chapter ? Who is xxx, yyy zzz and xyz ?

Don't forget to Vote and Comment.

I will meet you soon till then stay safe, take care and Love Yourself .

Byee Byee... Luv ya .

Published : 9 September 2023

Total Words : 2305 words .

Chapter 13

"What happened, Baby ?" Vincenzo frowned.

"Nothing. My stomach is upset. But as I am already late, I have to eat fast and that makes me frustrate and angry too." Bella said in hurry.

Salvatore chuckled.

"Babes, no one is going to say anything to you, you know ?" Salvatore asked, shaking his head.

"Yeah and if anyone says anything then just say them that you are Riccardo Russo's sister" Riccardo smirked.

He felt a smack on his head.

He groaned and glared at Salvatore.

"Why-"

"Not now, guys," Vincenzo said stopping them even before they could say anything "And What happened to your stomach ?" He directed his question towards Bella.

"I ate cookies at night so might be for that," She shrugged her shoulders and turned towards other two "Yes, stop fighting guys, you both are grown-ups. Behave like it. If you want, you can take some tips from me too" Bella sassed, rolling her eyes, and continue her eating.

Nancy, who just came there to take a dish, heard that and laughed.

Riccardo narrowed his eyes at her while Salvatore looked at her plainly. On other hand, Vincenzo laughed wholeheartedly.

"Sorry" Nancy mumbled a small apology before running in kitchen, still with a smile on her face.

Brothers sighed.

It's their regular life.

"Now you are not late huh ?" Riccardo glared at Bella, who just shrugged in response.

"You are becoming a naughtier day by day" Salvatore narrowed his eyes at her.

"And mature too" She stood up from her seat.

"You little-"

She squealed and ran inside the kitchen, before Riccardo could get her.

"She is so sassy" Riccardo huffed.

"And Savage too" Salvatore agreed.

Vincenzo chuckled and shook his head in amusement.

"Ric, are you going to drop her off at school ?" He asked him. Riccardo nodded his head.

"Drive carefully, Idiot" Salvatore said.

"Oh Sure, Idiot" He replied.

"Good-"

"Ok Enough, Idiots. She is right. You guys should take some tips from her" Vincenzo mocked.

Both of them shot glares at him.

"Let's goooooo, I am readyyyy" Bella said running towards them.

"Who is coming today ?" She asked looking at everyone.

"Your Favourite Brother, Babes" Riccardo said with a wide grin but his grin disappeared when he heard Bella's reply.

"Oh Sally, you are coming, let's go" She grinned mischievously.

Riccardo glared at her, playfully, while Vincenzo just chuckled.

"Oh no, Baby, I am not coming today. No worries, Ric will drop you off at school today. Bear with him today. Your favourite Brother will definitely come tomorrow." Salvatore said with sad smile, playing along with her.

Riccardo glared at him too.

"I will see you later" He warned his Elder brother, then turned towards his Bella "And you little munchkin-"

He said and lunged forward, picking her up in his arms, eliciting excited squeals and giggles from the little girl.

"Byee Bells, Take care." Riccardo smirked and said, "If someone bothers you, do you know what you should do ?"

Bella giggled. "Yes, I will kick them right in their guts."

"Yes, that's my girl !" Riccardo said, hugging her tightly and planting a kiss on her forehead. "Okay, now go."

"Bye, Ricc," Bella kissed his cheek and got out of the car.

She ran a bit inside but as soon as she reached the entrance, she turned around and looked back, giggling, waving her hand. Riccardo shook his head, chuckled, and waved at her. Bella laughed and ran inside the school.

Bella's footsteps echoed through the hallway as she made her way to her classroom. She entered her classroom, her heart pounding, and settled into her usual desk at the back of the room.

She had learned the names of a few classmates, and a couple of them had offered friendly smiles in the hallways. Today, Bella felt a bit more at ease as she settled into her desk, a sense of familiarity creeping in.

She's not the loner type; she loves making new friends. However, that doesn't mean she doesn't enjoy her own company. She relishes moments alone, immersing herself in her imaginative world.

The classroom buzzed with muted conversations as students chatted with their friends, their voices a comforting backdrop to Bella's thoughts. She gently tapped her pencil on the notebook in front of her, lost in her own world.

The door swung open slowly, and the teacher, Ms. Anderson, stepped into the room. Ms. Anderson was a tall, graceful woman with a warm smile that instantly put her students at ease. A hushed silence fell over the classroom, punctuated by the shuffling of papers and the occasional cough.

Ms. Anderson made her way to the front of the classroom, her steps measured and confident. The teacher's voice was gentle as she greeted the students, "Good morning, everyone." The response was a chorus of "Good morning" from the students.

"Take out your books, students"

As the teacher began the lesson, Bella's eyes glistened with curiosity. She sat upright in her chair, her small hands gripping her notebook, ready to absorb knowledge but her mind drifted to far-off places, to adventures yet to be had.

She tried to focus on her lectures but her wild imagination kept drifting.

In her daydreams, she could be a fearless explorer discovering hidden treasures in a jungle, or a brave astronaut soaring through the cosmos. Her imagination was like a vivid tapestry, and she wove it with the threads of books, novels, and fanfictions she couldn't wait to dive into.

While her teacher scribbled on the chalkboard, Bella's gaze drifted beyond the confines of the classroom window. She daydreamed about the cozy corner of her room, bathed in warm, golden sunlight, where her favorite reading nook awaited. The plush armchair, her loyal companion, beckoned her with open arms.

Occasionally, her teacher's voice would pull her back to reality, but Bella's daydreams were relentless.

The chime of the classroom bell jolted Bella back to reality.

"I should stop reading all these fanfictions." She sighed and stood up from her place.

"I am hungry. Let's go and eat something" She mumbled and packed her bag.

Bella entered the cafeteria and went to an empty table in the corner.

She took out her lunch box and immediately a smile crept on her face seeing a note with it. She opened it.

'A Sandwich with lots of love and kisses'

She giggled and shook her head at Salvatore's antics.

She started munching on it.

"Hey Bella"

Startled, Bella looked up from her box, her eyes meeting Alberto's. Her smile faded slightly as she studied the familiar face before her.

"Recognize me ? Your first friend from Eastway High School," Alberto grinned.

When did he become her friend ?

Bella blinked. Once. Twice.

"Hii" She smiled slightly.

He made himself comfortable beside her.

"So, How are you ?" He grinned. "Man, I've missed you so much; it's been 24 hours since we last talked," he sighed.

"Hey, let's do one thing, give me your number, and then we can talk all the time." His eyes sparkled with excitement as he happily made this suggestion.

On the other side, Bella was taken aback by this. She stared at him, her eyes wide with shock and her mind racing with questions.

she wondered, Why is he acting like they know each other for such a long time ?

Bella cleared her throat.

"Um, I don't have my phone with me. Sorry," Bella lied.

Alberto narrowed his eyes. "Don't lie; I know you have a phone."

Bella was taken aback. She distinctly remembered not taking out her phone in front of Alberto yesterday.

So how did he know she had a phone ?

Never mind, that's not the point. She can't give him her phone number.

She cleared her throat. "It's not my phone; it belongs to my brother. I can't give you the number."

"Okay Nevermind, I am giving you my number. Text me or Call me whenever you are free"

He said and pulled out a book from his bag along with a pen. He tore a piece from the last page of his book, scribbled something on it, and handed it to Bella.

When Bella looked, there were numbers written on it. She sighed and accepted it from him.

There is no way in hell she was going to call or even text him.

"You know Bella, we are friends but we don't know about each other. Let me introduce myself to you, properly" He grinned.

She so badly wanted to tell him that she isn't his friend. And she is not even interested. But, she can't.

What if he feel bad ?

"I am Alberto. Alberto Muratore. I am basically very cool guy. I never hurt anyone." He began.

Bella, despite her bewilderment, managed to offer him a slight, polite smiles, not wanting to be rude.

"My father is a rich businessman of the town. We own a mansion too. If you want you can come there too. I could buy this school if I wanted to-"

His words flowed freely as he spoke of himself in the most positive terms, behaving as though he were auditioning for the role of the school's most amiable student.

"- I am the most handsome guy here, you know. Girls just can't resist my irresistible personality. Well, you know, I've got that charm that seems to work with the ladies. I must be doing something right if all the girls seem to enjoy my company. It's like I have a fan club, and they're all girls ! I think I'm the unofficial 'heartthrob' around here." He said smirking at the end of his sentence.

"So that's why no one came to save you when you were getting beaten up ?" Before she could stop herself, these words just came out of her mouth.

Her eyes widened. She immediately placed her hand over her mouth.

What did she just do?

How could she say just like that?

She gulped a little.

On the other side, Alberto suddenly fell silent. His eyes darkened, and his jaw clenched tight. He even clenched his fist. "What did you say ?" Alberto asked slowly yet dangerously.

Bella immediately shook her head.

"What did you just say ?"

"Nothing" Bella replied softly, looking down.

He sighed.

"Listen Bella, I know you are uncomfortable since yesterday. But, forget about it. There's no need to get so offended by this. It's normal. And it's not like I said that I want to do Sex with you" Alberto said to Bella in a stern voice.

Bella's eyes widened again.

"W-What ?"

"And besides, you should get used to these things" Alberto added, rolling his eyes.

Bella gulped.

"What do you mean by this, that I should get used to these things ?" She asked him.

Alberto sighed.

"Leave it. We were on such a beautiful as well as an interesting topic but you just- ugghh ruin it." He mumbled annoyed.

Bella's head snapped towards him.

Bella was suddenly taken aback by his transformation.

The boy who had been speaking so sweetly just two minutes ago was now suddenly so angry. Why ?

"Well, never mind, I forgive you; you're so cute that's why I'm forgiving you" He suddenly pinched her cheeks making Bella slightly flinched due to sudden touch.

If she wasn't uncomfortable before, she is hundred and ten percent uncomfortable now.

"So, tell me about yourself" He said with a grin.

"Uh- My name is B-Bella. Bella Russo. I have three strong brothers" She said.

"Three Brothers ?" Alberto gasped a little.

"Hmm" She nods her head and looked down at her half-eaten sandwich.

She started eating it again.

Not wanting to appear rude, she extended her another sandwich towards Alberto. With a polite smile, she said, "Would you like some ?"

"No, I don't want it. My stomach is allergic to cheap foods; my Mom packed me something more high-class." He said Nonchalantly.

Bella gawked at him.

He refused Sally's sandwich; it's his loss, not hers.

"This is not cheap. This is actually the most delicious food of the world. Because, My Sally made this" She replied proudly.

Alberto chuckled.

"Cute. You are very cute. Be My Girlfriend" He blurted out, once again pinching her cheeks.

Her eyes widened in surprise, and her cheeks, already pink from the unexpected cheek pinch, turned an even deeper shade of crimson.

You are very cute. Be my girlfriend.

His words hung in the air, leaving her momentarily speechless.

"W-What ?"

She fumbled for words, her mind racing to comprehend what had just happened. It was as if the ground had shifted beneath her feet, and she found herself in an unfamiliar and awkward situation, caught off guard by Alberto's forwardness.

For a moment, she thought he might be joking, but when she saw the seriousness in his expression, she swiftly dismissed her initial notion that he was merely jesting.

Still, she asked "You are joking, right ?"

As if he suddenly realized the gravity of his words, he burst into laughter. "Yeah, yeah, I'm just joking." He laughed out loud.

However, Bella wasn't convinced at all. She couldn't understand why she didn't feel like he was joking. It was as if she could see through his lies. As if she could see through his laughs.

"Ok Ok, enough joking. Now tell me more about you" He said, after his mini laughing session came to an end.

Overwhelmed by fear, startlement, and an intense sense of discomfort, Bella didn't waste a moment.

"Uhm- I have some work." She immediately stood up from her chair swiftly excused herself from the uncomfortable situation.

Bella made her way out of the still busy cafeteria, totally unaware of two pairs of eyes watching her.

Her heart pounding in her chest. She came out of the cafeteria and ran towards the washroom.

She needed a moment to collect herself and process the unexpected turn of events.

What just happened ?

<<°>>~<<°>>

Classes went in blur.

Whole time her mind is occupied with Alberto's words.

You are cute. Be my Girlfriend.

He told her he was joking but why Bella's heart is not ready to accept it ?

Did Bella do the right thing by saving Alberto ?

Should she have done that ?

Was Alberto telling the truth about Mark and Teo ?

Or was Alberto at fault ?

Suddenly, a car pulled up in front of her, and the blaring horn jolted Bella out of her thoughts. She blinked rapidly, her focus shifting from Alberto's enigmatic behavior to the present moment. Her brother, Salvatore, sat behind the wheel.

Bella wasted no time. She eagerly hopped into the passenger seat with a smile adoring her face.

"Hey there, Babygirl" Salvatore smiled.

She immediately leaned in and kissed his cheek, with a grin.

He chuckled and kissed her forehead.

Bella settled comfortably into the car's plush seats, fastening her seatbelt with a practiced click. The familiar scent of the car's interior, a mix of leather and Salvatore's favorite air freshener, enveloped her. She watched as her brother started the car's engine with a gentle purr, a subtle hum that signaled the beginning of their ride home.

As the car pulled away from the school, Bella began to recount the day's events and again Alberto's words started roaming in her little mind.

Am I thinking too much ?

What if Alberto was really joking ?

Who knows, maybe he just wants to be friends, and I'm overreacting ?

"What's going on inside your little mind ?" He asked her, the steering wheel spun swiftly in his hands as he expertly took each turn, keeping his eyes momentarily on Bella. He frowned when she doesn't replied.

"Bella," Salvatore said, his eyes on the road ahead, his grip on the steering wheel tight. Her head snapped towards him.

"What ?"

He sighed.

"You seem a bit off. Is something bothering you ?"

Bella stared at him for a minute, her fingers fidgeting with her dress as she mustered the courage to tell Salvatore, about what had happened earlier.

She hesitated for a moment before taking a deep breath. "Well, something did happen today," she admitted, her voice trembling slightly.

Salvatore shot her a concerned glance, his brow furrowing. "What happened, Bella ? You can tell me."

Bella recounted the incident with Alberto, her voice quivering as she spoke. "Well, Alberto, he...he jokingly proposed to me, Sally"

Salvatore's jaw clenched visibly, and his grip on the steering wheel tightened even more. His protective instincts kicked in, and he struggled to maintain his composure. "He did what ?" he asked, his voice low and intense.

Bella sighed.

"Yeah, I-I mean he told me that he was j-joking but I don't know why I still felt- I mean It made me really uncomfortable. I didn't know how to react."

"Did he do anything else ?" He gritted his teeth.

"No," Bella continued, her gaze fixed on her lap, "but what if he was just joking, Sally ? What if I'm overreacting ? I don't want to make a big deal out of it if it was just a prank."

Salvatore's face remained hardened, but he softened his tone for Bella's sake. "Bella," he said, his voice filled with concern, "your feelings are valid. If something makes you uncomfortable, it's important to express that. Alberto should know better than to make jokes like that."

Bella looked up at her brother, her eyes filled with uncertainty. "I just don't want to cause any drama, Sally. I don't know if I should say anything."

Salvatore sighed, his protective instincts still at the forefront. "Bella, your well-being and comfort come first. If you're uncomfortable, then tell him that you are uncomfortable. And remember, it's never wrong to stand up for yourself when something makes you uncomfortable."

"But what if he was just jok-"

"No Bella, that's wrong. There is a difference. If a joke is making you uncomfortable, then it ceases to be a joke. You should let him know that you're not comfortable with it. Don't second-guess yourself by worrying about whether he'll feel bad or sad; always trust your instincts. Follow your guts. If you're feeling uncomfortable, you're feeling uncomfortable-no second thoughts. The next time he does something like this, you will express your feelings. You will tell him that you are uncomfortable." He explained.

Bella listened to him carefully.

Salvatore couldn't help but notice the somber expression on her face. He glanced over at her, and said softly "Remember, We'll always support you no matter what. You have your Vinny, Riccy and your favourite man of the world - Sally always with you."

She smiled softly.

"But my favourite man is Riccy" She smiled cheekily.

Salvatore narrowed his eyes.

"You little girl-" He poked her side, getting a chain of adorable giggles.

"Still Riccy is handsome- ahh" She giggled when he again poked her side.

Salvatore couldn't resist tugging playfully at her ponytail, messing up her hair. Bella let out a whine, her face breaking into a giggle.

With a sly grin and a mischievous glint in his eye, Salvatore decided to take an unexpected turn. His grip on the steering wheel tightened, and he abruptly turned it to the left, making the car veer in the opposite direction from their house.

Bella frowned.

She couldn't help but express her confusion.

"Where are we going, Sally ?"

Salvatore, his eyes focused on the road ahead, responded with a playful wink. "Well, I thought we could use a little treat to lighten the mood. How about some ice cream ?"

Bella's eyes twinkled.

Bella's initial puzzlement gave way to a delighted surprise as she realized they were heading to an ice cream shop. Her mood began to lift, and she couldn't help but cheered with a joy.

Salvatore pulled the car to a stop in front of a charming ice cream shop. It had a colorful sign, and the sweet aroma of freshly made ice cream wafted through the air. He and Bella stepped out of the car and walked into the cheerful shop.

Inside, the shop was adorned with colorful posters and had a vibrant atmosphere. Bella's eyes sparkled with excitement as she took in the array of flavors displayed in the glass case. She walked up to the counter, where a friendly ice cream vendor greeted them.

"Can I have a scoop of chocolate chip cookie dough, please ?" She said politely with a grin on her face.

Salvatore, standing beside her, observed Bella's choice with a warm smile. He then made his own selection.

"I'll take a scoop of pistachio, please."

"Sure Sir" Vendor said and immediately handed them their respective ice creams.

After receiving their ice cream cones, Salvatore and Bella found an available table near the window. They settled into their seats.

"Yumm" She moaned after eating first bite of her ice-cream.

"You know what, Sally? The government should include ice cream in a balanced diet. Every meal should contain ice cream. Without ice cream, your meal is incomplete. And those who don't eat ice cream with meals should be subjected to hefty fines. At least this way, Vinny will have to allow me to have ice cream every day. Just imagine, ice cream with breakfast in the morning, ice cream with lunch in the afternoon, ice cream with dinner at night-nothing but ice cream all day. It will be so much fun, life will be completely set !" She ranted dreamily.

Salvatore laughed wholeheartedly at that.

Bella and her wild imaginations always amused him.

"Wait, let me inform Vince that we've come for ice cream. Otherwise, he'll have a sword hanging over my neck !" Salvatore shuddered at the thought and took out his phone to message Vincenzo.

Bella laughed at that.

Salvatore focused on his phone to message his brother, his attention momentarily diverted.

Bella was savoring her chocolate chip cookie dough ice cream, sipping on the sweet nostalgia of childhood. She moaned with every bite.

Ice creams can always lift mood.

She took another spoonful of her ice cream, enjoying the dessert.

But then, something unexpected caught her attention. An old man.

An old man sitting a few tables away was staring at them more precisely at her intently.

She frowned slightly as she glanced behind her to check if anyone was there, but there was no one behind her.

Bella met his gaze, and for a brief second, their eyes locked. In that fleeting moment, she thought she saw a smirk on the old man's face. It sent a shiver down her spine, making her feel uneasy and uncomfortable.

"Bella" She snapped out.

"What happened ? Where did the smile on your face suddenly disappear to ?" Salvatore asked her playfully.

Bella looked at him and again looked behind him but to her surprise no one was there. No old man. Her eyes widened.

Is she hallucinating ?

Where did that man go ?

She gasped.

She is literally seeing things.

"Babes, what happened ?" Salvatore asked, concerned.

"N-Nothing, I guess, I am going to be mental patient soon, Sally" She sighed dramatically.

He narrowed his eyes.

"Why ?"

"I guess, I am watching things. For a second, I thought I saw someone there staring at us." She replied pointing behind Salvatore. His face turned serious.

Salvatore immediately turned around.

He looked around at everyone, but he didn't see anything unusual, so he turned back towards Bella.

"Did you see his or her face ?" He asked her, seriously.

"He. He is a man. Actually an Old man. But I didn't see his face properly. It was just for mere second" She explained.

He nodded, thinking about something.

"Leave it, Sally, I am just being paranoid" She sighed dramatically again.

He chuckled and shook his head.

"My baby is learning new words, huh ?" He smirked.

She whinned at that and he laughed.

<<°>>~<<°>>

"Just a few days left now. Then my good days will come. I won't have to eat this poor people's food anymore. I'll have money too. After getting the money, I'll first repay all my debts, then I'll live in a big mansion, then I'll get treatment for my illnesses, then I'll travel the world-"

"Shaira" a man shook her.

"What ?" She snapped.

"Snap out of your dreams" He glared at her.

"Why ?" She glared at him back.

He sighed and back down.

"Because it's not that easy, Shaira"

"What do you mean ?" She glared at him.

That man sighed.

"I am scared. I saw her today. She is looking so happy with them"

Shaira tilted her head. A glare turned into a smirk. An Evil Smirk.

"Oh. Not for long. It's time to call him"

"But what if-"

"No what ifs. Everything will be fine. I will make everything fine. After all, this is a matter of 450 billion Euros. And when it comes to money, I can do anything."

Shaira smirked.

"Oh, Vincenzo Russo, you won't be able to do anything. I'll take your daughter right from under your nose, and you won't be able to do any-thing, just like you couldn't do anything thirteen years ago." She whispered with a smirk.

She laughed out loudly.

"I will come in your life, soon"

To Be Continued...

Longest Chapter till date. First time crossed 4k+ words.

You guys like long Chapters, right ?

I Expect more comments in this chapter (if you can, then only. Not forcing)

So tell me what do you think about the chapter ? Alberto ? Old man ? Shaira ?

Little Preview :

Xxx : I am not even asking you. I am telling you. Stop being a brat and do as I said. (Growl)_______________

Yyy : Bruises may toughen the skin, but they don't heal the soul.________ __________

Zzz : Take care of her. She is too naive. And while eating icecream, she looks cute too.________________

Guess people...

Don't forget to Vote and Comment.

I will meet you soon till then stay safe, take care and Love Yourself .

Byee Byee... Luv ya .

Published : 13 September 2023.

Total Words : 4320 words .

Chapter 14

A /n : I know I am late. I am quite busy with my studies and submissions. So, as a compensation, here is the chapter with 5k+ words. Hope, you guys will forgive me. Please I expect lots of inline comments in this chapter. I will upload Epiphany tomorrow (maybe). Till then, Enjoy....

"What ?"

"What the fuck ?"

Vincenzo clenched his fist in anger, while Riccardo just wanted to punch something very badly.

The room bore the weight of their collective determination, and a palpable tension hung in the air.

"Hmm. But Relax, I already told her to tell him that he is making her uncomfortable" Salvatore sighed.

"And you think he will listen to her ? Ridiculous" Riccardo scoffed.

"I want his each and every detail about that boy" Vincenzo ordered in coldest voice.

"Name : Alberto Muratore, Age : 15 years old, Studying in Eastway High School. Average performance at school. His Father Roberto Muratore is the owner and CEO of Muratore Industries. However, Muratore Industries has been struggling financially and here are his other details." Salvatore ended, handing a file to Vincenzo.

"Leave these shits, let me handle this" Riccardo gritted his teeth.

"And how will you handle all of this ?" Salvatore raised his eyebrow.

"I will make him regret his life decisions" He snapped.

"Ric, you are going to beat him ?"

"Of course, he deserves it"

"Ric, Be practical, you can't just beat a 15 year old boy" Salvatore snapped.

"Sal, you be practical, I can beat 15 year old boy" He argued back.

"Stop thinking from your fist, use your fucking brain, Riccardo"

"Sal, I am seri-"

"ENOUGH" Vincenzo slammed his hand on the desk infront of them.

"Ric, Sal is right. You can't just go and beat that 15 year old boy. He is basically a teenager" Vincenzo said sternly.

"But Vince we can't let go of this matter. First that boy asked her about her periods and Sex and now he asked her to be his girlfriend. This is not a little thing, Vince. We can't treat this like it's nothing serious" Riccardo argued, furiously.

How could his elder brothers even think like that ?

"Ric, I am not saying that we are gonna forgot about this." Vincenzo said and turned towards Salvatore.

"Call Mr.Muratore. Let's have a nice chat with him" He smirked.

Before anyone could react, the main door of the meeting room creaked open gently.

Their heads snapped towards the intriguer, with confusion written on face.

There stood a little girl with a pout on her lips, and sleep in her eyes.

Bella.

Each and every expressions changed.

Vincenzo's stern countenance softened, and a warm smile tugged at the corners of his lips. Salvatore's smirk transformed into a genuine grin, and he raised an eyebrow inquisitively. Riccardo's anger dissolved into a wide toothy smile.

The icy aura of the room gave way to an unexpected warmth.

"What happened, Bells ? Why didn't you sleep yet ?" Vincenzo asked opening his arms.

Bella immediately ran in his arms.

"Vinnyyyy" She whinned hugging him.

His arms wrapped around her delicate form, encompassing her entirely. Her head nestled into the crook of his neck as she hugged him, and her tiny hands rested gently on his broad back. Vincenzo's muscular arms cradled her body with a sense of love and care.

"What happened, Baby ?" He asked gently, stroking her hair.

"My Stomach is aching" She whispered tightening her hug.

He slightly frowned and made her comfortable in his arms. He turned her sidewise in his lap and gently rubbed her tummy.

"Is it from yesterday ?" He asked concerned. She nuzzled more in his neck, seeking comfort. He could see the sleepiness in her eyes.

"I don't know" She muttered.

He sighed and held her close.

"Did you eat anything else after dinner, Bells ?" Salvatore asked sitting infront of them.

She shook her head.

"Don't worry it will be okay" Vincenzo said as he rubbed her tummy. His fingers traced soothing circles on her soft skin, applying just the right amount of pressure to alleviate her discomfort. Bella's eyes, tired from the pain, slowly closed, and a small, contented sigh escaped her lips.

Vincenzo continued to rub her tummy in a rhythmic motion, his protective instincts kicking in as he watched over his precious little girl. The room was filled with a sense of love and serenity, as Bella's pain began to ebb away.

Eventually, Bella drifted off to sleep, her head resting gently on Vincenzo's chest. He continued to stroke her tummy, kissing her head multiple times.

Salvatore couldn't help but be moved by the sight. He took out his phone discreetly and snapped a quick picture of Bella and Vincenzo sharing that intimate moment. His eyes sparkled with affection as he captured the image, wanting to treasure this sweet memory of their love. A soft smile played on his lips, reflecting the warmth he felt for his Bella and the pride he had for Vincenzo's loving care.

On the other hand, Riccardo simply admired the duo. His heart swelled with admiration for his elder brother Vincenzo and the unwavering love he showed to Bella. He realized in that moment that he had incredible role models in his family, and he cherished the bond they all shared.

As Salvatore clicked the picture, Riccardo muttered "Send me that too"

<<°>>~<<°>>

"BELLA"

Bella turned around only to see her technically first friend of Eastway High school.

Alessia.

"Heyy Alessia" Bella greeted with a grin on her face.

Alessia smiled genuinely.

"What's up, girl ?"

"Nothing much, just heading to the library," Bella replied "What about you ? Where are you going ?"

"Ohh I am going to staff room. Miss Grace has some work" She shrugged her shoulders with a smile on her face.

"Where have you been all these days ? I didn't see you at school." Bella asked out of curiosity.

"Oh, I went to New York. We had a family function there, that's why."

She replied.

"Oh ok"

"Bella"

"Yes ?"

"Can I ask you one thing ?" Alessia reluctantly asked.

Bella tilted her head in confusion.

"Yes ?"

"I've been hearing some rumors lately. Is it true that you're in a relationship with Alberto Muratore ?" She asked slowly.

Bella's eyes widened, and her cheeks flushed crimson in bewilderment. She stammered, "Wha-what ? Alberto ? No, I'm not ! Where did you hear that from ?"

Alessia maintained her friendly smile, sensing Bella's discomfort. "Oh, you know how gossip spreads around here," she replied casually. "But I wanted to hear it from you directly. So, you're not dating Alberto ?"

Bella shook her head vigorously, her surprise gradually turning into a mixture of embarrassment, discomfort, awkwardness and frustration. "No, Alessia, I'm not dating him. Heck, We're not even friends. I don't know how these rumors started."

Alessia chuckled softly, reassuring Bella, "Alright, I figured it was just a rumor. Don't worry too much about it. People say all sorts of things."

Relief washed over Bella's face as she realized that Alessia didn't mean any harm with her question.

"Thanks Alessia. I didn't even know such a rumor existed." Bella sighed.

Alessia smiled "It's ok. It happens. By the way, Bella, have you met Alberto yet ?"

Bella stiffened at that question. Her eyes widened slightly as she recalled her encounter with Alberto.

What is she supposed to answer now ? She can't say that he made her uncomfortable. What if Alessia is Alberto's friend and not like how she described him ?

She doesn't want Alessia to feel bad, so she decided to just give her vague answers.

"Yes, I did meet him" She replied with a slight smile.

"What do you think of him ?" Alessia narrowed her eyes.

Bella slightly gulped, "He seems friendly enough."

Alessia's expression turned more serious as she leaned in closer to Bella. "Listen, Bella, You seem very sweet to me, that's why I'm telling you something, I want to give you a piece of advice. Alberto, well, he's not exactly what he appears to be. He has a reputation for flirting with girls, and he's been involved in some drama in the past."

Bella was taken aback by this revelation. She couldn't figure out whether she should be happy that Alessia isn't Alberto's friend or sad that Alberto isn't a good guy. Of course she had sensed a flirtatious vibe from Alberto but hadn't known the extent of it.

"Oh, I didn't know that. Thanks for telling me." Bella nodded, with a smile on her face.

Alessia nodded, her gaze unwavering. "I don't mean to gossip, Bella, but I've seen too many girls get hurt by falling for his charms. It's better to stay away from him and be cautious."

Bella appreciated Alessia's candor and concern for her well-being. She nodded, her gratitude evident in her eyes. "I'll keep that in mind, Alessia. Thanks for looking out for me." Of course, she is not going to fall for him.

Alessia patted Bella's shoulder reassuringly. "You're welcome, Bella. Just remember, there are plenty of great people to be friends with here. Don't let one person's reputation cloud your experience."

Bella nodded and smiled gratefully.

"Ok, I am going now. Byee. Take care" She smiled and left from there.

Bella's footsteps echoed softly in the hushed, book-lined aisles of the school library. The library embodied a harmonious fusion of tradition and contemporary design. Upon entering, one was greeted by rows of tall bookshelves. Each shelf was neatly organized, housing an extensive collection of books. In the center of the library, clusters of modern, ergonomic seating arrangements beckoned students to gather for study sessions or contemplative reading.

Bella noticed that today was unusually quiet in the library. There were just one or two students scattered at different tables, engrossed in their studies. A pair of girls sat together, huddled over textbooks, sharing notes in soft voices. Another student sat alone, her headphones on, immersing herself in the world of her laptop.

At the circulation desk near the entrance, the librarian, a middle-aged woman with kind eyes, meticulously organized books, occasionally glancing up to offer assistance to anyone in need.

She hesitated for a moment before heading towards a pile of books on the shelf. Her heart yearned for the solace of her favorite book, 'To Kill a Mockingbird' by Harper Lee.

Bella found an empty table near a sunlit window and opened the book, hoping that its familiar words would provide solace. The book had always been a refuge for her, a place where she could hide from the reality. Yet, today was different. Alessia's warning about Alberto weighed heavily on her mind.

In the pages of her cherished book, Bella found echoes of the moral dilemmas that Alessia's warning had stirred within her. Scout's innocent perspective on the world and Atticus's unwavering sense of justice had always resonated with her. But now, they took on a new significance as she tried to reconcile these ideals with the complex reality of Alberto.

Bella remembered how Scout, a character in her book, was always curious and kind to others. She thought that maybe she could use Scout's approach to understand Alberto better instead of making quick judgments about him. She wanted to be open and empathetic, just like Scout. However, Bella couldn't shake off Atticus's strong dedication to doing what's right. She wondered if she could be as principled as Atticus while dealing with the new challenges and began to think if she should be more careful in her interactions with Alberto.

Her eyes flitted across the pages, but her mind was elsewhere, locked in an inner battle. On one side, there was the comfort of her beloved book, a story that spoke of empathy and understanding. On the other side, there was Alessia's warning, urging her to be cautious of Alberto.

However, amid this inner turmoil, she failed to notice that she remained alone in the library.

Unbeknownst to her, Someone had entered the library. His presence remained unnoticed amidst the rows of bookshelves. He approached Bella's table, with angry and blazing eyes. He stood before her, waiting for her to acknowledge his presence, but she remained lost in her book.

The seconds ticked by as Bella continued to read, unaware of the storm brewing right in front of her. His anger simmered, his patience wearing thin. Finally, unable to contain his emotions any longer, he cleared his throat loudly, causing Bella to startle and look up, her book momentarily forgotten.

"A-Alberto" She stuttered, gulping slightly.

"What did you say to your brother ?" He gritted his teeth. She frowned slightly.

"What ?" She stood up from her chair.

"I asked you what the fuck you told to your brother about me ?" He glared at her. Bella would be lying if she said she isn't scared because she is scared.

"T-That-"

"THAT I FUCKING MADE YOU UNCOMFORTABLE ?" She flinched due to sudden yell.

He took a step forward towards her.

She gulped looking around her only to find no one is there.

Where did everyone go ? Even the librarian isn't here.

She gasped when she suddenly felt his cold hands held her soft arms.

 Triggered Warning : Trying to Harass Sexually

Bella's heart quickened its rhythm, the rush of adrenaline coursing through her veins. Her once-composed eyes widened considerably. The natural flush of color drained from her face, leaving her complexion noticeably pallid. Her breath caught in her throat. As her gaze instinctively lifted, it met Alberto's visage, contorted with anger, sending a jolt of apprehension through her

"You are going to regret it" He whispered, lowly. A chill raced down her spine, causing goosebumps to erupt on her skin.

"Alberto l-leave- me-" She whispered trying to pry his hands of her arms. He tightened his hold.

He chuckled humourlessly "Leave you, huh ? Well, you see, you complained to your brother, and he told my father. My father is disappointed in me. I can't tolerate that. You took action, and now you deserve a consequence. As your punishment, you are going to be my girlfriend."

Bella's fear intensified, gradually escalating into a growing sense of panic. Her chest tightened, and her heart pounded erratically, as if trying to break free from its confines.

Suddenly a smile crept on his face. A smile that churned everything in her stomach. Breathing became a struggle; her inhalations were shallow and rapid, while her exhales were uneven and tremulous. She felt an oppressive weight on her chest, as if an invisible hand had clenched around her lungs, making it difficult to draw in air.

"N-No pl-please-" She struggled in his hold but he just kept on tightening his hold. Her eyes filled with tears as her hands began to tremble.

"Yes, I will make you regret" He gritted his teeth leaning towards her.

Bella's eyes widened in fear. Her thoughts raced, a whirlwind of anxiety and confusion. The library, once a sanctuary of serenity, now felt like a claustrophobic trap.

She could feel his breath fanning her face.

Her eyes welled up with tears. She didn't want this; it was the last thing she wanted. Her voice became trapped in her throat, as if a lump had formed, rendering her unable to speak. She longed to shout, but her body refused to obey. It was as though her entire being had frozen in place, paralyzed by the overwhelming situation.

Bella's heart raced, and a sense of helplessness washed over her. In that terrifying moment, all she wanted was to escape from the impending situation, to return to the safety and comfort of her brothers' embrace.

Just Kick them in their guts.

Riccardo's words echoed in her mind.

Mustering her all strength, she delivered a forceful kick to Alberto's shin, a sharp and unexpected blow that caught him off guard.

Alberto's grip on her arms faltered, and he recoiled in pain, a sharp groan escaping his lips.

"You Bitchh" He groaned.

Bella took deep breaths before started running out of the library but Alberto was fast. He immediately grabbed her back of the hood again forcefully yanking her back.

"AHHHH LEAVE ME" She shouted, struggling to free herself from his grip.

"Stop struggling. You belongs to me. You are my girlfriend" He scowled trying to nuzzle his face in the crook of her neck.

Tears rolled down her cheeks as she try to free herself from his hold.

"N-No pl-please-leave m-me-" She cried.

"No. Never. I will make you mine. Yesterday I asked you to be my girlfriend but you took it as a joke now I am telling you to be my girlfriend" He restrained her movements by holding her hands tightly, definitely leaving bruises there.

She sobbed uncontrollably.

"Noooo leave me, Alberto"

"Now be a good girl and let me taste your soft lips, baby" He said seductively, in her ears, making her disgusted.

She shook her head immediately trying to free herself from his grip.

"N-No pl-please-leave m-me- I can't P-Ple-ease-" She stammered with fear.

"I am not even asking you. I am telling you. Stop being a brat and do as I said" He growled, again leaning in trying to kiss her on her lips.

She immediately shut her eyes with tears rolling down on her cheeks.

Just as his lips were about to meet hers, a sudden and powerful fist connected with his face.

"AAAHHHH"

The force of the blow stunned Alberto, causing him to stumble back, clutching his injured face. He screamed loudly holding his face.

Bella was immediately yanked away from Alberto's hands and pulled in someone's chest. She found herself enveloped in a comforting, warm embrace, her trembling form pressed against someone's chest.

She sobbed hard as she could heard a soothing voice trying to comfort her.

"Sshh it's ok, you are ok, calm down" She heard a familiar warm voice. A hand, caressed her hair softly trying to calm her down but this just made her cry more. She cried heavily, her sobs a release of pent-up fear and anxiety.

She recognise this voice.

Mark.

Yes.

She knows that she'll be very embarrassed after this, but right now, all she needs is comfort. Surprisingly, she feels safe in Mark's arms.

His arms held her tightly, offering a reassuring security.

Bella clung to him, her trembling form finding solace in his comforting presence. His steady heartbeat served as a soothing rhythm, calming her frayed nerves.

Eventually, her breath gets even as she calmed down.

With all her courage, she turned her head a little only to witness a dangerous scene infront of her.

Teo is beating the living daylights out of Alberto. She could see that Alberto can't even keep his eyes open. He is already lying in his pool of blood. She immediately turned her head away from the scene infront of her.

Mark's hold tightened around her.

"Teo Enough. Leave him" Mark said but Teo didn't hear him.

"Teo, Leave him, she is already scared" He shouted sternly. Teo's hands stopped in his tracks. He looked at her and his eyes softened. He left him with one last kick and came towards them.

"Are you okay ?" He cleared his throat and asked softly.

Bella pulled out from the comforting hug and looked down, slowly nodding her head.

"Thank you" she muttered slowly. They glanced at each other.

"Guys, let's get out from here first" Mark said and they left from there leaving unconscious Alberto there.

<<°>>~<<°>>

"Nancy, Bring me the water" Vincenzo ordered, sitting on the couch.

He don't know why but he is feeling restless since morning.

Throughout the morning, Vincenzo felt really uneasy. It was like something was bothering him, and he couldn't ignore it. It felt like a heavy burden on his mind. He loosened his tie, allowing himself a small measure of relief. The cool air from the air conditioner provided some respite as he adjusted the settings to make the room more comfortable. He leaned on the couch as he closed his eyes trying to shake off that feeling.

Nancy approached with a glass of water and he accepted it and downed it in a single gulp, hoping to quench not just his physical thirst but also the nagging feeling of disquiet that had settled within him.

"Sir, Are you Okay ?" Nancy asked Slowly.

Vincenzo sighed and said "Yes, Nancy. Don't worry. I am fine. Where are others ?"

"Salvatore Sir is in office and Young Master is in his college and Bella is in school" She replied.

Vincenzo nodded.

"Make their favourite lunch today" He ordered and left from there to his office room.

He entered in the office, and adjust the air conditioning, lowering the temperature. He removed his coat and casually tossed it onto the couch, and sat on the plush chair behind his desk. He sighed.

Why am I feeling so strange ? Is everything okay ? I hope nothing has happened to anyone-

Before he could think anything, a phone rang quickening his heartbeats for a second.

He frowned seeing the unknown number blinking on the phone screen.

He pressed green button and put it close to his ear and said in his regular deep cold voice "Hello"

"Hello, My dear Nephew and husband"

<<°>>~<<°>>

"I am S-Sorry" Bella muttered looking down.

Teo and Mark looked at each other.

"Why are you apologizing ?" Mark asked gently. She looked up. Their hearts break seeing tears in her eyes.

She is just a kid. A 12 year old. It's not easy for her. She just went through one of the cruelest act of the world. Someone just tried to kiss her. Someone just tried to harass her. She just got sexually harassed. She doesn't deserve this. Heck, no one deserves this.

"I-I- fought with you b-because of him and now y-you fight with h-him for me" She stuttered trying her best to control herself. She just wants to go back in her Vinny's arms. She just wants to cry on her brothers' chest. She just want them to comfort her. Nothing else !

"Don't apologize. Its not your fault. Alberto is always like this. He is always a little fucker. That day when you protected him from us, we were not bullying him, instead he was harassing a girl" Mark said.

Bella's head snapped towards him.

"What ?" Her mouth ajar opened. Did she literally protect a boy who was harassing a girl ?

"Did I literally protect a boy who was harassing a girl ?" She voiced out her thoughts.

They slightly chuckled at her cute face and nodded.

"I am really a little brain" She muttered, slapping her forehead. She shook her head and looked at the boys infront of her.

"I am so so sorry. I really misunderstood you guys and scared you that day. Please don't get scared of me. I will never make such moves on you guys" She told them, seriously.

They looked at her face for a second and glanced at each other and as their eyes met, they laughed out loud.

She frowned. "What ? I am not joking. Why are you guys laughing ?"

"You think you scared us that day ? You are very funny, little girl" Mark laughed out loud pinching her cheeks. Bella glared at him.

Bella doesn't like it when anyone other than her brothers pinches her cheeks, and after coming to this school, someone pinched her cheeks again. But yes, the way she felt uncomfortable when Alberto touched her, she didn't feel the same discomfort when Mark touched her cheeks.

While, Teo and Mark laughed wholeheartedly seeing her glare.

"Stop it" She glared at them.

"Ok ok" They controlled themselves.

"Good" She scoffed. They smirked.

Before she could say anything, her gaze drifted to Matteo's clenched fists, and her heart skipped a beat as she noticed the bruised and swollen knuckles. A gasp escaped her lips as realization washed over her, and she felt a surge of guilt welling up inside her.

They frowned seeing her change of expressions.

"Your hand is b-bruised. I am sorry" She said, pointing towards Teo's hands. She couldn't help but blame herself for Teo's injuries. After all, he had fiercely confronted Alberto to protect her. They looked at where she was pointing.

"Oh, its nothing" He waved his hand like nothing happened.

But Bella royally ignored him and slid her bag from her shoulder and placed it on the ground. She unzipped the bag and reached inside, her fingers searching for a small, familiar item. She took out a band-aid.

She hesitantly extended her hand, her fingertips barely grazing Teo's bruised knuckles. She winced slightly at the sight of it.

He must be in so much pain just because of me.

She thought as her eyes glistened with tears.

Gently, she began tending to Teo's bruises.

Unknown to her, both boys looked at her with pure amusement in their eyes. She is truly a child.

Her movements were careful and tender as she applied the band-aid to the injured knuckles.

"It will be fine now, Teo" Bella said softly.

"It's not hurt that much by the way, anyways Thanks" Teo shrugged.

"Your knuckles are literally bruised" Bella exaggerated, with wide eyes.

"So ? Remember what I told you last time ? Bruises are necessary. It makes you strong. Underneath every bruise lies the power to heal and the courage to endure." Teo said.

Bella looked in his eyes.

"But leaving them untreated doesn't make you strong. And, Teo you know, Sally says, Bruises may toughen the skin, but they don't heal the soul" She said proudly.

This made him shut up.

Mark cleared his throat and asked trying to avoid awkward silence.

"Who is Sally ?" He asked.

"Sally is my brother. He is very handsome. Actually, all my brothers are very handsome. But, I enjoy teasing them, so I always tell them they're not handsome" She giggled at that.

"How many brothers do you have ?" Mark raised his eyebrow.

"3. I have three brothers. Vinny, Sally and Riccy. I love all of them." She said smiling widely.

"That's cool" Mark replied with a smile.

"What about you guys ? Are you and Teo brothers ?" She asked them, curiously.

"First of all, Do you know our names ?" Teo asked, raising his eyebrow. She nodded.

"Mark and Teo" She replied.

They sighed.

"Nope, I am Matteo. Matteo Giuseppe Romano and he is Marco, Marco Leonardo De Luca"

Bella gawked at them.

"oh"

"Yes" They nodded.

"And no, we are not brothers but we are more than brothers" Marco replied.

Bella gasped "You guys are dating ?" Her eyes sparkled.

Their eyes widened. Matteo looked disgusted. While, Marco looked shocked.

"No" Matteo immediately denied, "I am straight. Even if I weren't, I still wouldn't have dated him."

"Exactly, I am straight too. And what the fuck you mean by saying you wouldn't date me ? What's wrong with me ? I'm so handsome, I have muscles, a great body, what else do you need ?" Marco replied, offended.

"A brain. which you don't have. And secondly, I have my own standards; I can't just date any random brainless person" Matteo rolled his eyes.

"Excuse me, are you really calling me a Brainless person ? Don't forget, I scored higher than you in the last exams" Marco retorted.

"Yeah ? And how much higher have you scored ? Just half mark more, right ?" Matteo smirked.

"Still, that counts and that proves that I am not a brainless person, you are"

"Of course, you are not a brainless person, you are a brainless idiot"

"You know what, fuck off. If I weren't straight, I still wouldn't date you. Even if you were the last person on Earth, I still wouldn't date you." Marco glared at him.

"Thank God, I am-" As the two engaged in their spirited banter, Bella couldn't help but burst into genuine, wholehearted laughter. She found their bickering amusing. It reminds her of her brothers' bickerings. Her laughter filled the air, making both of them glare at her but she can't stopped her laughing.

Her laughter was infectious, and soon Matteo and Marco, their egos momentarily set aside, couldn't help but join in. The area was filled with the sound of their genuine laughter.

Meanwhile,

At house,

Vincenzo clenched his fists.

"How dare you to call me ?" He gritted his teeth.

Shaira chuckled.

"Aww, dear little boy, why are you angry ? Didn't you miss me ?"

Vincenzo tightened his jaw.

"By the way, I must say, My daughter is very pretty, huh ? Of course, I am her Mother. She takes after me for sure"

"Stop it, Bitch. She is not your daughter. She is my daughter. Only mine. Don't ever call that innocent yours. She has nothing with you"

"Aww, protective huh ?" She laughed, "But who knows about the future ? Today, she may want nothing to do with me, and tomorrow, she may want nothing to do with you. Who knows what will happen when she learns about what her dear Vince has done with her mother, how he kept her away from her mother. Just Imagine, How much she'll come to hate you ?" Shaira said dreamily.

Vincenzo's eyes darkened.

"And do you think my daughter will trust you ? You'll speak, and she'll believe you ? Don't forget, Shaira, She is my daughter. She will choose me, over everyone else" Vincenzo replied.

"Well then, take care of her. She is too naive. And, while eating icecream, she looks cute too." Vincenzo's breath hitched.

So, Bella was right when she told Salvatore that she saw someone in icecream shop.

"What-" Before he could say anything, she interrupted him.

"And you're right. She will trust you, but just imagine what she'll think when she finds out that her strong Vince couldn't even protect himself in front of a girl." Shaira laughed out loud.

To Be continued...

I am expecting lots of comments in this chapter. And of course, I will expect. Because even after being busy with studies, and submissions, I am writing chapters for you guys. I am trying my best to not to disappoint you guys. So, of course, I will expect something from you guys too, right ?

Anyways, tell me if you guys like the chapter or not ?

Little Preview:

Xxx : Oh My God, what should I do now ? *Panic*__________________

Yyy : What happened ? Why are you looking so tensed ? *Concerned*________________

Zzz : Bella. Come here. *Stern*__________________

Xyz : I-I am s-sorry- P-Ple-ease-forgive m-me- *Crying*______________

Guess .

Don't forget to Vote and Comment.

I will meet you soon on Saturday till then stay safe, take care and Love Yourself .

Byee Byee... Luv ya .

Published : 20 September 2023.

Total Words : 5130 words .

Chapter 15

- -

There are different types of Emotions in the world, but right now, what Vincenzo is feeling the most is anger.

Vincenzo Russo - The Great And the most Successful Business Tycoon of the country, who is especially known for his calmness in every situation is now sat with disturbed mind. His usually tranquil mind resembled a turbulent sea, its calm surface now shattered by the storm of emotions that had been unleashed. Thoughts raced through his head like a chaotic whirlwind, and the usual clarity he possessed was clouded by a maelstrom of anger, fear, and confusion.

Shaira's voice, dripped with venom, echoed in his ears, provoking a storm of emotions within him.

Her voice rang in his ears.

Who knows what will happen when she learns about what her dear Vince has done with her mother ?

His grip tightened on the paperweight.

How he kept her away from her own mother ?

Just imagine, how much she'll come to hate you ?

Vincenzo's eyes darkened as his fists tightened more, knuckles turning white as his face contorted with anger. His brows furrowed, and his normally calm eyes now blazed with fiery intensity. The memories that Shaira's words had awakened, old wounds that had never truly healed, seared through his mind. His breath came in heavy, controlled exhalations as he fought to maintain his composure.

Just imagine what she'll think when she finds out that her strong Vince couldn't even protect himself infront of a girl ?

His breath hitched as all negative thoughts started coming in his mind.

Beneath the anger, a deep, gnawing fear lurked. His heart raced, thudding loudly in his chest. The thought of his precious 12-year-old daughter, Bella, hating him sent chills down his spine. He imagined her innocent face, her laughter, and the warmth of her hugs. It was an image he couldn't bear to lose.

What if, Shaira was right ?

What if Bella will really-

His eyes widened as his chest tightened. Vincenzo's office suddenly felt suffocating. His chair creaked as he pushed himself away from the desk, his legs trembling slightly as he stood. He paced the room, his mind racing with thoughts of what if's. Each step he took mirrored the turmoil within him, his movements agitated and restless.

The paperweight still gripped in his hand, he couldn't shake the feeling of helplessness that overwhelmed him. The desire to hide his daughter from the cruel world, clashed violently with the knowledge that his past had resurfaced to haunt him. His anger raged like an inferno, but beneath it all, fear clawed at his heart, threatening to consume him.

Vincenzo's knuckles turned crimson as his grip on the paperweight tightened further. He could almost hear Shaira's wicked laughter echoing in his mind. The emotions warred within him, a tempestuous storm of anger and fear that threatened to engulf him. In that moment, all he wanted was to ensure himself that he will do anything to make Bella forgive him, even if it meant confronting the ghosts of his past that had returned to haunt him.

His head snapped towards the door which just opened with a large thud.

Salvatore comes inside with a disturbing look on his face as his face held a frown.

Before Vincenzo could react anything, Salvatore asked, "Where's your phone, Vince ? Why aren't you answering your phone ?"

Vincenzo frowned and looked at the phone on his desk.

"Why ? What happened ?"

He asked slightly panicked, suddenly his instincts kicked in.

Salvatore looked in his eyes.

"It's Bella"

<<°>>~<<°>>

"Our Librarian found this boy Alberto badly bruised in the library. According to her, only your sister, Miss. Bella was there at that time, Mr. Russo. He is in critical condition, Mr.Russo. Here, Mrs. Muratore wants to file a complaint against your sister, as she was the only one who was present there at that time."

Bella's head snapped towards the Principal as her eyes welled up.

Vincenzo clenched his fist and glared at the principal.

He turned towards Bella and his eyes softened.

He motioned her to come towards him and she immediately came near him. He hold her hands, softly caressing her knuckles.

"What happened ?" He asked her, looking in her eyes.

Tears rolled down her cheeks as her voice got caught in her throat.

"Don't worry, I am with you" Vincenzo whispered in a soft voice, immediately reassuring her.

"What will she say ? Her tears themselves prove that she harmed my son. Principal, please call the police immediately; this girl deserves punishment. She has hurt my innocent child so badly." Mrs.Muratore growled, glaring at Bella.

Bella, on other side, flinched due to harshness of the voice. She was with Matteo and Marco on terrace, when she heard the announcement of her name being taken like she was needed in Principal's office as soon as possible. When she came here, she saw a lady, with some revealing clothes, makeup and high heels sat there, furiously glaring at her.

She gulped when she came to know about everything.

"Sweetheart, look at me" Vincenzo cupped her face in his large hands making her look in his eyes.

"What happened Baby ?" He again asked softly.

"Oh God, she is too annoying, I just want her behind the bars-"

Her voice caught in her throat when, Vincenzo's head suddenly snapped towards her. His eyes darkened as he glared at the lady, dangerously.

Mrs.Muratore gulped a little.

"N-No N-No I d-don't want to g-go to j-jail, Vinny- n-no- P-Ple-ease - trust m-me- I-I-"

Vincenzo immediately pulled her in his embrace.

"Sshhh calm down, Baby. You are not going to jail. No one can separate you from me, baby. Calm down, please, take a deep breath" Vincenzo's soft voice made her calm down slightly but still her tears are rolling down her cheeks.

He continuously rubbed her back softly.

"I-I- H-He hurts me, Vinny- I-I-"

"LOOK AT THE AUDACITY OF THIS BIT-"

"One more word, Mrs. Muratore and I will show you who will go behind the bars" Vincenzo gritted his teeth. His eyes darkened at the lady infront of him.

His hands are comforting his daughter right now that's why the lady infront of him is standing there without any Bruises.

But, he will make sure that she will get what she deserves.

"Bells, look at me" He cupped her face and made her look in his eyes.

Bella's teary eyes met his warm one.

"Do you trust me ?" He stared in her teary eyes, hoping to hear 'Yes' from his daughter.

And without any hesitation, she immediately said "Yes"

Vincenzo sighed in relief which goes unnoticed by everyone.

"Then, tell me everything" He said in a gentle tone.

Bella gulped, "V-Vinny, I was in l-library reading a book when suddenly A-Alberto came there, h-he yelled at me because I told you about him and you c-complained to his Dad, h-he was so angry th-that h-he held my arms t-tightly. It was painful, Vinny. H-He tried to k-kiss m-me- V-Vinny- so, I k-kicked h-him. But then, he a-again tried to k-kiss m-me-" She sobbed hard.

Vincenzo's eyes hardened as his jaw tightened. He is not even angry. Neither Furious. He is Fucking Livid.

On another side, his heart brokes. This world is so cruel. The thing which happened to him 12 years ago is going to happen to his own daughter now ? Why History is repeating itself ? What his innocent Bella did to anyone ? What he did to anyone ?

"Bullshit. Fucking Bullshit. Principal sir, she is lying. To save herself she is lying. You tell me, if she is telling truth then how the hell my son is injured ? Who hurted my son ? Why the hell librarian found my son badly bruised and unconscious on the ground ? Tell me, Principal, who beat my son-"

"I did"

Each and every head present there snapped towards the new source of voice.

Bella looked at the door with her teary eyes. There stood her new friends, Marco and Matteo, with a cold neutral look.

Mrs. Muratore frowned but then glared at them.

"What do you mean ?" Principal asked them.

Matteo turns towards Mrs. Muratore.

"I beat your son. He is lying on the hospital bed because of me only"

"What the fuck-" She glared at them and raised her hand to slapped him but before her hand could touch Matteo, Vincenzo held her wrist.

His eyes are darkened. He slightly pushed Matteo behind him and took a step forward towards her.

"I told you Mrs.Muratore, one more word and I will show you who is going to be behind the bars."

He turned towards Bella.

"Bella, go out with them. I will be back" He ordered sternly.

"No wai-" Vincenzo's glare turned towards the Principal who immediately stopped himself from saying anything.

"Now" He again ordered, still glaring at the Principal.

Bella nodded and three of them came out from the cabin.

He turned towards the lady who is now looking like a sweating hell.

"You fucking dare to call my sister bitch ?"

His fist clenched.

He so badly wants to punch the lady. But he controlled himself.

Mrs.Muratore gulped a little.

"Call the fucking police, now, principal" Vincenzo said, in deep voice sending shiver down their spines.

Lady's eyes widened in shock.

"NO, You can't call the police. You don't have any proof against my son. I-I- will file a case against you both brother and sister. My son is a v-victim here." She said frantically.

Vincenzo smirked.

"You want to file a case against me and my sister, hmm ? Ok then go ahead. Call police. I am waiting" Vincenzo said and sat on the chair, keeping his right leg on his left leg, like a king he is.

Mrs. Muratore frowned. Her shaky hands started dialing the numbers when suddenly she flinched due to someone barged through the door.

"I am sorry, Mr. Russo. P-Ple-ease forgive us, please forgive my son, please Mr. Russo, please, I am begging you, please, please please" A man immediately bend down, joining his hands infront of Vincenzo.

Mrs. Muratore gasped.

"Honey, what are you doing ? Why are you begging to this Bastard-" She asked her husband.

"Shut up, Gianna. Do you even know who is he ?" He snapped towards his wife.

Mrs. Muratore aka. Gianna scoffed.

"Of course I know, Roberto, do you even know what his sister did-"

"Oh Gianna, for God sake, shut up," He turned towards Vincenzo, who was just looking at the scene with a smirk on his face, "Please, forgive her. She is an Idiot. Please forgive both of them. please I am begging you"

"But Roberto, your wife wants to file a case against me and my sister" Vincenzo said.

Roberto's eyes widened as his head snapped towards his wife.

He immediately stood up and glared at his wife.

"What ? Are you out of your mind or what ?" He asked her harshly.

Gianna looked at her husband in disbelief.

"Seriously ? Roberto, he is going to put our son behind the bars and you are trying to defend him ?" Gianna glared at him.

"He could, Gianna. Because our son is not a victim here. He did a mistake and that's why I am apologizing to him on behalf of our son"

"Shut up Roberto. There is no proof against my son. I am not letting anyone touch him. I will surely file a case against this man and his sister-"

"SHUT THE FUCK UP GIANNA. DO YOU EVEN KNOW WHO IS HE ?"

Gianna looked at Vincenzo up and down and smirked.

"Probably working in some company. But he don't know who is he messing with"

"Gianna he is not working under anyone. Instead I am working under him" Roberto yelled.

Gianna froze.

What ?

Her eyes widened.

"What ?" She muttered.

"Yes. He is Vincenzo Russo. The Great Business Tycoon of the country. Our company is under him, Gianna. If he wants he could take everything from us. That's why I am telling you to shut up. Please for God sake, just stop your mouth" Roberto whispered at the end.

All the colours drained from Gianna's face as she looked at Vincenzo's smirking face. She gulped.

"B-But Roberto, they will send Alberto to j-jail-"

"Don't worry, I am doing something-"

"Enough" They slightly flinched and looked back.

Vincenzo stood there with a blank look.

"Enough of your drama. And you, you want proofs, right ? See this video" He extended his phone towards the couple.

The couple looked at each other.

"What ? Here is the proof, Mrs. Muratore. See this"

With a shaky hands, Gianna took a phone and play the video.

Her eyes widened when she saw that her son is admitting each and every thing he did with Bella in these days.

Gianna gasped in horror as her eyes welled up.

She immediately looked at Vincenzo.

"I-I- am s-sorry- please forgive my son. P-Please don't call police." She joined her hands.

Vincenzo looked at them emotionlessly.

"I don't fucking need your apologies. Say sorry to my Sister, not me. And I am not calling police because your son is just a 15 year old kid. But don't forget, what he did is not a mistake, it's a crime. I don't want to ruin any kid's future. That's why I am leaving him." Vincenzo said in cold tone.

Roberto's eyes sparkled. He smirked unnoticably.

Wow, he melted. I just shed a few crocodile tears, and he melted ? That's good. Thank God, my child is safe. How many times have I told that scoundrel that forcing himself on a girl isn't the issue for me, but he should consider her family for once. I thought we were done for this time. My business would have been shut down if Vincenzo had taken any action.

Roberto thought and sighed in relief.

"Thank you so much, Sir, thank you so much." He said happily with a grin on his face.

"I am not done, yet, Mr. Muratore."

Grin disappeared from Roberto's face.

Vincenzo took his phone and dialed a number and keep it on his ear.

"Salvatore, Prepare a formal legal notice stating that B.R. Corporations is hereby terminating all business associations with Muratore Industries. Make sure, that this legal notice is promptly dispatched to their company headquarters, along with a demand for the complete settlement of all outstanding debts owed to B.R. Corporations."

Roberto's face paled while Gianna gasped.

His eyes widened.

"N-No M-Mr. Russo, you can't do that. You just told me that you are forgiving my son and now you- N-No pl-please-"

Roberto pleaded.

Vincenzo looked at the man infront of him with emotionless eyes.

"Your outstanding debt currently stands at 3000 million Euros with an interest rate of 50%. You are required to settle this debt by repaying a total of 4500 million Euros within the next two weeks. Failure to meet this obligation within the stipulated time frame will result in the acquisition of your company by B.R. Corporations, and your personal assets, including your residence, will be subject to legal action, including potential seizure"

Gianna's eyes widened in shock.

Roberto's breath hitched, he immediately bend down holding Vincenzo's legs. Tears rolling down his cheeks.

"P-Please S-Sir, you can't do this. M-My family, my c-company, e-every-thing is on line. Everything will be ruined, P-Please don't do this, Mr.Ru sso, I am begging you- please-"

He cried.

"You should have thought about all this when you didn't teach your child to respect girls." Vincenzo replied coldly.

"I am sorry, Sir, I am really sorry. B-But I promise sir, Alberto will never ever s-show his face to your s-sister, Sir, please forgive him, P-Please"

Vincenzo clenched his fists.

"That's where you are wrong, Muratore. I am not only talking about my sister. I am talking about every girls that became your son's prey in past."

"B-But Sir, those girls are poor. They don't have money and you are also a boy, please think about it, boys have needs." Roberto said.

Vincenzo's eyes darkened.

He couldn't believe that these type of people are also existing in the world. He looked disgusted.

"So, you think it's ok to touch poor girls without their consents, just because they have no money ? Disgusting. They are humans too. They have rights too. But guess what, you will learn that when you will be in their situation and trust me, it will be soon"

Vincenzo gritted his teeth and turned towards the Principal who is watching all the scene with a nervous eyes.

"I am the new trustee of this school and I want CCTV cameras in each and every corner of the school except Washrooms and changing rooms. Get that in your mind" He glared at the principal, who frantically nodded.

Vincenzo again looked down at Roberto.

"Two weeks, Roberto, only two weeks"

<<°>>~<<°>>

"Are you okay, Bella ?" Marco asked her, concerned.

Bella bit her lips and nodded.

"Thank you" She muttered.

They nodded.

"By the way, who was he, Bella ?"

Marco asked curiously.

"Vinny. My Eldest Brother" She muttered looking down.

The boys formed an 'O' shape with their mouths.

"Bells"

Bella's head snapped towards the source of the voice and her eyes widened.

"Sally" She immediately jumped in his arms. He held her close to himself and close his eyes in relief.

From the moment, he heard the news from the school, he wants nothing but to hold his Bella close to his heart.

Feeling a homely warmth, she couldn't control herself and tears started rolling down her cheeks as she cried.

"Sshh it's ok, calm down, you are my strong girl, right ?" Salvatore asked her rocking her like a baby. She nodded, still sobbing.

"Then, don't cry, Babes." He cooed at her.

"S-Sally, she said that she will send me j-jail-"

"No princess, no one could send you anywhere. Do you really think we will allow that ? Do you really think your Vinny could live without you ? Do you really think your Sally will let anything happen to his munchkin, huh, tell me ?" He whispered in her ears, trying to calm her down.

She sniffled and shook her head.

"Then ? Vinny is in office, right ? He will manage everything, don't worry" He kissed her forehead.

She nodded and snuggled in his shoulder.

Salvatore felt her behaviour little off but shrugged it off.

"By the way, do you really think that your Riccy will leave his poopy princess alone ? Huh ?" He teased her, trying to lift up her mood and as a result, she whinned and glared at him.

He laughed at that.

Eventually she calmed down and her eyes dropped due to exhaustion.

Salvatore noticed the two boys who were just standing there looking at the siblings with adoration.

He chuckled.

"What's your name, kids ?" He asked them.

Matteo cleared his throat.

"I am Matteo Romano"

"And I am Marco De Luca. Nice to meet you, Sir"

Salvatore formed a 'O' shape.

So they are the boys, Bella was talking about.

"Nice to meet you too, guys. Thank you so much to stay with her when she was alone" Salvatore said softly.

They smiled and nodded.

"You're welcome, Sir, she became our friend in such a short time. She is really good" Marco replied smiling.

While, Matteo nodded.

Salvatore smiled.

These boys are good.

Vincenzo came out of the cabin gaining every attention.

"Is she ok ?" He immediately asked.

Salvatore nodded.

He sighed.

"That fucker tried to kiss her" Vincenzo cursed, glaring at nothing.

Salvatore looked at his elder brother with sad eyes. He knew, that his brother's old wounds had resurfaced.

"Vince, she is okay. See, calm down" He gently pat his back.

Vincenzo took a deep breath and nodded.

"Did Ric come ?"

Salvatore smirked.

"He is on his way from the hospital"

Vincenzo sighed.

"By the way, it's very clever of you, huh. Sending Ric to the hospital to make a video of that boy"

Vincenzo smirked at that.

<<°>>~<<°>>

"Agghh it's again paining"

A groan left from Bella's mouth as she stirred in her sleep.

She changed her side hoping to sleep peacefully but her stomach is aching, hurting her.

Her hands started rubbing her belly as she curled up in her bed, trying to catch some good sleep.

"I think I should go to washroom" Mumbling to herself, she sat on her bed lazily. Mustering her all courage, she stood up and dragged her feet towards her washroom. Her eyes are still closed.

Removing her pants, she sat on the comode and sighed.

Her closed sleepy eyes suddenly widened when she noticed the red liquid.

She gasped.

Did she get her first periods ?

Her hands flew towards her mouth in shock. She is no longer sleepy now.

It all makes sense now. Stomach aching from two days, suddenly a pimple on her cheek, mood swings. Yep, she gets her first period.

"Oo I am really foolish. Why didn't I notice all these signs ?" Bella said, slapping her forehead in frustration.

"Oh My God, what should I do now ?"

She panicked.

"I should call Vinny B-But it's too embarassing. Oo God, what should I do now ? I can't tell my brothers just like that. It's too embarassing. Think something, Bella, think somethin-"

"Yepp Nancy Aunty. Yes, she could definitely help me. Yes, I should call her" Bella nodded.

She kept some tissue papers on her underwear and wore it. After flushing and washing her hands, she immediately came out from her room.

"Why did my period have to come now ? Couldn't it have waited a little longer ? Ugh, that's why my stomach has been hurting for the past two days. My back and legs ache too. Oh no, does this mean I have to endure all this pain every month ? Oh no, just thinking about it is stressing me out already. It's a good thing I was at home when it started. What if it had happened at school ? Or in the class ?Or in the car ? Oh no, how will I manage this every month ? I don't even have pads with me. Oh, shoot, I need to hurry, maybe Nancy aunty can help me, I hope she doesn't leave home. She is the only one who could save me from this right now- Oww, can't you see where are you going ?" She snapped, rubbing her forehead when she bumped in someone's chest.

"Woah Princess, so moody huh ?" Riccardo narrowed his eyes.

Bella's eyes widened as she froze in her tracks.

Moody ? Did Ric find out that she is on her periods ?

No. It's impossible.

Riccardo frowned.

"Are you ok, babygirl ? What happened ? Why are you looking tensed ?" He asked her.

She sighed in relief.

"N-No, I am ok, Ric and I am really sorry for snapping at you." Bella immediately looked down, sadly.

Riccardo's eyes softened.

"Cheer up kiddo, it's ok" He ruffled her hair.

"Anyways, I want-"

"Ric, I am sorry, I will talk to you later, I am in hurry right now, ok ? Sorry" She pleaded with her puppy dog eyes and ran out from there before he could even react anything.

"What happened to her ?" He frowned but shrugged muttering something like teenagers these days.

Meanwhile, Bella immediately ran towards the kitchen, forgetting cramps.

She sighed in relief when she saw Nancy is there in kitchen washing utensils.

"Aunty" She panted.

Nancy turned around.

"Bella ? What happened ?" Nancy frowned.

Bella looked here and there.

"Aunty, please can you give me pad ? I am on periods" She whispered.

Nancy stared at her dumbfounded.

"Oh wait" She immediately washed her hands and took out her bag from one cabinet and took out a pad from that bag.

"Here"

Bella immediately took them. Without a second thought, she hugged her and ran from there thanking her multiple times.

<<°>>~<<°>>

"I can't hide this from others. I have to tell them. Yes, you can do it, Bella, you can do it. Go ahead." Giving herself a pep talk, she knocked on the door hoping to see her eldest brother in his room.

Her eyes widened in shock seeing everyone there.

"Come in, Bella" Vincenzo smiled at her.

She smiled back. A little forced.

"N-No it's ok. I will come later. Byee" She turned around to leave but a voice stopped her in her tracks.

"Wait Bella. Turn around." Riccardo called her.

She gulped and turned around.

"What are you hiding ?" He narrowed his eyes.

Bella froze in her place.

Salvatore and Vincenzo frowned at that.

"What are you saying, Ric ?" Vincenzo asked his brother, looking at Bella.

"She is definitely hiding something from us-" And he told them how she behaved suspiciously earlier too.

Vincenzo stared at her for a minute.

She stood there froze, looking nervous as hell and he immediately knew, she is definitely hiding something.

"Babes, what happened ? What are you hiding ?" Salvatore asked her gently.

She gulped and shook her head.

"Hey Babygirl, why are you nervous ? We are here, right ? Come inside first of all" He gently said her but she didn't move an inch from there.

"Bella, Come here" Her head snapped towards the source of the stern voice.

She looked at Vincenzo with her doe eyes.

Without a second thought, she came inside the room.

"Sit" He told her sternly. She immediately sat on his bed.

"Now tell me what is happening ? Why are you looking nervous ?" He asked her. His tone was gentle now.

She gulped.

What she is supposed to say now ?

How will she tell these people that she's started her periods ?

How will she explain this to them ?

She gulped when she saw their concerned, curious eyes.

"Vinny, I-I- am- I mean I started-" what started ? Oh God, this is too embarassing.

"Baby, look at me" Vincenzo called her softly.

She looked in his eyes.

"Are you uncomfortable with us ? If it is so, then no need to. We are your brothers, Bells. We love you. There is nothing in the world you can't share with us" He cupped her face.

She stared in his eyes and sighed.

She is not uncomfortable with them. She could never.

"Vinny, I started my periods today." She mumbled out.

"What are periods ?" Riccardo asked Salvatore, who in response just smack his head.

Riccardo gasped when he realised what he just heard. His head snapped towards his Little girl. His eyes widened like a saucer.

Salvatore blinked in surprise. Once. Twice.

While, Vincenzo's hands froze. His eyes widened slightly too. It's not that Vincenzo is unaware of periods. He knows about periods. And he is prepared for Bella, but he just hasn't realized that his daughter is growing up so fast.

Bella's cheeks flushed with embarassment seeing the expected reactions from them.

But before she could say anything, Vincenzo came out from his shock State.

"Oh My God you are on your periods and you are telling me this, now ? Are you even serious ? What do you need for it- I am an Idiot. What am I even asking ? I am sorry I will bring everything. Baby, is it hurting anywhere ? Oh God, do you need anything like Chocolates, icecreams, hot water bag, medicines anything ? Do you want to go to doctor ? Why are you silent ? Is it hurting that bad ? Please say something, Bella. Oh God, Sal, take out my car, we are going to hospital right now-"

"Vince. Stop it" Salvatore kept his hand on his eldest brother shoulder.

Vincenzo stopped. His eyes widened.

Did he just rant infront of his family ? Oh God, this is too embarassing.

He looked around only to see Riccardo and Bella in total shock.

"Give her a time to reply, Vince" Salvatore said, trying to fight a smile.

Vincenzo cleared his throat and again looked at his daughter.

"You. What are you staring at ? I am asking you something. Answer me" He narrowed his eyes.

Bella came out of her shock.

"I am okay, Vinny. Yes, my tummy is hurting but not too much. It's ok. And yes, I need chocolates and many icecreams. But no, I don't need Doctors and medicines. It's natural so of course No doctors and I heard that we should try to avoid medicines for the cramps." She said.

"How do you know all of this ?"

Riccardo asked for the first time.

She rolled her eyes.

"Because, I never slept in my class" She smirked cutely.

Riccardo glared at her while other two burst out in laughter.

"Good one, babes" Salvatore winked at her.

"Oh whatever" Riccardo rolled his eyes. A slight smile on his face.

"Jokes aside princess, but what did you do ? Where did you get the pad from ?" Vincenzo asked, worriedly.

"Nancy Aunty helped me, Vinny" She cheekily smiled.

Vincenzo sighed in relief.

"Thank God. But, you should have tell us, Bells. Nothing is there to hide, Babes. Periods are natural. Nothing is there to feel embarass." Salvatore said softly.

"We understand that you might feel uncomfortable in telling us-"

Before Vincenzo could complete his sentence, Bella immediately lunged forward and hugged him.

"No. I never felt uncomfortable with you guys. Never. You guys raised me. You know me better than I know myself. I-I- just I don't know I guess I was just too nervous" She mumbled softly.

Vincenzo hugged her tightly and kissed her head.

"Are you really ok, tho ?" He mumbled softly.

She nodded and sighed.

Salvatore and Riccardo looked at the duo with adoration.

Bella pulled out from the hug and stood up but soon gasped when she saw a red stain on Vincenzo's bed. Her eyes widened.

"Oh no, Vinny, I-I- am s-sorry- Please forgive me"

To Be Continued...

Really really really really sorry for such a late update. A whole Month. I am so f*cking sorry. Please forgive me, guys. Please...... .

I get my days off for some days, I will try my best to give early updates... I will try my best.

Again sorry for late update.

Don't forget to Vote and Comment.

I will meet you soon till then stay safe, take care and Love Yourself .

Byee Byee... Luv ya .

Published : 6 November 2023.

Total Words : 5085 words .

Chapter 16

"I want chocolates"

Bella whinned umpteenth time today.

"Bella, you can't eat chocolates now. It's dinner time" Vincenzo told her.

"Vinny pleaseeeee" She pouted.

"Ok, first eat your food then Ric will give you chocolates, ok ?" Salvatore asked her.

She pouted more.

She don't know what is happening with her. But right now, she is getting terrible mood swings.

When she saw stains on Vincenzo's bed, her eyes welled up because of guilt. She apologized many times until Riccardo practically picked her up and left her in washroom.

While, Vincenzo on other hand panicked seeing stains on his bedsheet. He immediately left to the nearby grocery store and literally bought half of the store.

One moment, she just wants to cry while another moment, she felt angry.

"Eat Bells" Riccardo reminded her.

Sulking, she took a morshel and put it in her mouth unwillingly.

They chuckled slightly seeing her sulking figure.

"Why are you sulking like a cat ?" Riccardo narrowed his eyes.

"Because I can't sulk like a buffalo. Because you are a buffalo" She muttered, taking another bite.

"What the hell ? Do I look like a buffalo to you ? Oh please go and do an eye-check up, princess" Riccardo rolled his eyes.

"Oh, My eyes are perfect, Mr. Prince, infact you go and do a brain check up" She replied.

Riccardo looked at her in disbelief but before he could say anything,

"Ok Enough kids. Stop bickering and eat your food" Salvatore announced.

"Oh hello, I am not a kid." Riccardo retorted back.

"Still, behaving like a kid-"

"Enough Bella" Vincenzo scolded her sternly. She pouted and continue eating.

She looked up only to see Riccardo smirked at her, in response she just poked her tongue out. He chuckled at her childishness.

<<°>>~<<°>>

"She get her periods, Shaira"

Shaira smirked at that.

"That's cool. Time to call Vincenzo"

<<°>>~<<°>>

"What happened Bella ? Why are you crying, Baby ?" Vincenzo asked panicked.

He entered in her room only to see his precious daughter curled up on the floor, crying her eyes out. His heart dropped as he immediately crouched near her.

He pulled her in his arms and hugged her immediately.

She curled up on his lap and sobbed.

"What happened Princess ? Please say something. Why are you crying ? Is it hurting anywhere ? Should I call doctor ? Hmm ?" He asked her, panicked.

She shook her head, crying more.

"Then what happened ? Why are you crying ? Do you want anything ?" He asked her.

"Riccy" She mumbled, crying.

He frowned.

"Ric ?"

She nodded, rubbing her eyes.

"Should I call him ?" He again confirmed and she nodded.

"Ok wait" He immediately took out his phone and dialed his number.

He picked up in second ring.

"Vince, we are literally living in a same house. If you are missing me this much, just come to meet me, bro" Riccardo said, before Vincenzo could say anything.

Vincenzo sighed.

"Shut up- oww what happened ?" He immediately looked down at Bella, when she literally smacked his chest.

Bella glared at him with her tearful eyes.

"Don't scold him" She pouted.

Vincenzo rolled his eyes at that.

"Sure" He could hear his brother's laugh on another end.

"Riccardo, can you please come to Bella's room ?" He slightly mocked.

"Oh yeah sure, why not" Riccardo smirked and hanged.

Here, Vincenzo kept his phone and again hugged her.

"He is coming. Now tell me what's happened ? Why were you crying ?" He asked her.

She pouted and rubbed her eyes.

He gently removed her hands from her eyes, "Don't do this"

"I am here- what happened ?" Riccardo immediately asked seeing Bella's red puffy eyes.

Bella immediately jumped in his embrace and he caught her.

"I am s-sorry- Riccy, I h-hurt y-you-" She sobbed hard.

Riccardo frowned immediately hugging her in his embrace and looked at Vincenzo in confusion who in response frowned too.

"Babes, you didn't hurt me. Please calm down. I am ok, see" Riccardo rubbed her back, gently.

"I-I- called you b-buffalo- sorryy" She cried harder.

They both looked at each other in confusion.

"Don't worry guys, it's because of hormones" A voice called. They all looked at the door.

Salvatore entered.

"Bells. Look" He called out. She sniffled and looked up at Salvatore. Her teary eyes lit up when she saw a chocolate bar in Salvatore's hand.

She smiled and took it from him.

"Thank you", She muttered and tore its wrapper.

"Heyy give me too" Riccardo tried to take a bite. She immediately hid it behind her back and glared at him.

He looked at her in total disbelief.

A moment before she was crying and apologizing and now she is glaring.

She wiggled out from his hold and stood on the ground.

"I will give you. Don't steal." She muttered, breaking a bar in four unequal pieces and keep a biggest piece for herself and gave other three to them.

Vincenzo and Salvatore smiled and shook there heads.

Bella glared at them.

They immediately took a piece.

She turned towards Riccardo and extend her hand with a chocolate but before he could take, she closed her fist, "First tell me that you forgave me."

Riccardo raised his eyebrow.

"Don't you think, babes, that this is not a way how you should ask for forgiveness ?" He smirked.

"Did you forgive me or not ?" She challenged him, crossing her arms on her chest.

"Umm ... No ?" He decided to tease her.

"I will eat this" She tried to threaten him.

"Ok. Go on. Eat it" He smirked.

"I am not joking, Ric, I will really eat this" She glared at him.

"Ohh Babes, I am telling the same thing, go on eat it" He grinned knowing very well that Bella will never eat it.

And as expected, her eyes brimmed with tears.

"Ouch" Riccardo winced as Salvatore smacked his head.

While, Vincenzo immediately pulled her in his embrace.

"Don't cry Bells, he is just joking, look, look, he is just joking" Vincenzo points towards his brother. She looked at him in tearful gaze. While, Riccardo grinned.

"You are so bad" She glared at him with a teary eyes.

"Sorry Babes" He laughed and took him in his embrace.

She feed him his piece and hugged him tightly.

He laughed out loud, hugging her back tightly.

They don't know what's actually happening with her. At one moment, she is excited, and then next second she is inexplicably angry and irritable. Whole day, they literally watched her went from laughing to crying to snapping at them within minutes. One thing is for sure that she is having terrible mood swings.

When Vincenzo came to know about Bella's periods, realization hits him. He realized that his precious little girl is now growing up. He felt a complex mix of emotions. He is proud that his daughter is growing up well. Raising her singlehandedly, he couldn't help but feel happy. Seeing her giggling in Riccardo's arms, made him relieved that he protected her innocence really well. Seeing her happy, made him forget all his pain, grief, everything. Hearing her giggles is the best thing to his ears. And he will do everything in him to protect these adorable giggles.

On other hand, Salvatore is adoring his little princess. Seeing her growing up is making him feel like he is raising her. He loves her like his own. She is his first child, whom he raised. Watching her grow up, he couldn't help but be amazed by how his Bella had become a matured, beautiful yet a cute girl. She is going to turn lots of heads and that's for sure. He sighed. He is not ready for this at all.

While Riccardo had already planned in his head how he would torture any boy who even dared to look at her. He was ready to gouge out the eyes of anyone with ill intentions towards his Babes, and there was no doubt that he would stop at nothing to do so.

They all came out from their trance because of a phone ring.

Vincenzo frowned looking at the unknown call. He excused himself and came out from the room.

Biting his lip, he picked up the call.

Keeping it on his ears, he said "Hello".

His throat dried off as his face drained of any colour when he heard the voice on the call.

"Well, I heard My Daughter is growing up. How cool, isn't it ? Guess what, now she has the capability to carry a baby too."

To Be Continued...

Short and boring chapter, I know... But trust me, drama is on it's way ;)

Please point out my grammatical mistakes.

I hope you like it btw ... .

Don't forget to Vote and Comment.

I will meet you guys soon till then stay safe, take care and Love yourself .

Byee Byee ... Luv ya .

Published : 8 November 2023.

Total words : 1485 words .

Chapter 17

"So, what do you want to watch ?"

"Frozen, pleaseee"

"That's too girly"

"Then, 365 Days"

"Heyyy, there is no movie with this title"

"Ok, what about 50 shades of grey ?"

"Oh God Bella, who is teaching you all these things ? Please stop hanging out with those rowdy boys" Riccardo exaggerate, cupping Bella's face.

Bella giggled.

"Nuh-uh, they are nice" She replied cheekily.

Riccardo rolled his eyes.

It's been 2 weeks. Everything is going well. No news from Shaira. Business is going perfect. College is going smoothly as well as School is going good. I mean that's what they thought.

"Let's just watch Frozen" He grumbled.

Bella giggled.

He set everything, pressed play and movie started.

Riccardo lounged on the couch. As Elsa's childhood unfolded onscreen, he maintained a skeptical expression, occasionally glancing at his phone.

"You know Ric, Elsa has magical ice power" Bella beamed, eyes fixed on the screen.

He smirked, tapping his phone screen, "Magic ? Wow."

According to him, all these magical stuffs are childish. He is not at all interested in watching these princess or magical stuffs. But, for her sake, he was watching the movie, more like boringly scrolling through his phone.

However, as Elsa revealed her ice powers during her coronation, Riccardo couldn't help but raise an eyebrow.

He narrowed his eyes, watching intently as Elsa inadvertently revealed her ice powers.

"Let it goo~" Bella's eyes sparkled.

Riccardo, still maintaining an air of nonchalance, couldn't help but glance back at the TV when Elsa belted out "Let It Go."

The snow glows white on the mountain tonight~

Not a footprint to be seen,

A kingdom of isolation,

And it looks like I'm the queen,

Bella sang along, totally engrossed in movie.

The wind is howling like this swirling storm inside,

Couldn't keep it in, heaven knows I tried,

Don't let them in, don't let them see,

Be the good girl you always have to be,

Conceal, don't feel,

don't let them know,

Well, now they know,

Bella squealed and immediately spread her arms just like Elsa and sang,

"Let it go, let it go~"

Can't hold it back anymore

Let it go, let it go~

Turn away and slam the door

I don't care what they're going to say

Let the storm rage on

The cold never bothered me anyway~

Bella flipped her hair sassily, singing last line making Riccardo rolled his eyes playfully.

It's funny how some distance makes everything seem small

And the fears that once controlled me

can't get to me at all

It's time to see what I can do

To test the limits and break through

Bella shouted at the top of her lungs, "No right, no wrong, no rules for me

I'm free

Let it go, let it go~

I am one with the wind and sky

Let it go, let it go~

You'll never see me cry

Here I stand and here I stay"

She again squealed when Elsa tapped her foot on the snow.

Let the storm rage on~

Riccardo slightly leaned in, as his eyes stuck on the screen when a castle is suddenly built on the snow.

My power flurries through the air into the ground

My soul is spiraling in frozen fractals all around

And one thought crystallizes like an icy blast

I'm never going back, the past is in the past~

Bella sang loudly,

"Let it go, let it go~"

And I'll rise like the break of dawn

Let it go, let it go

That perfect girl is gone

Here I stand in the light of day

Let the storm rage on

The cold never bothered me anyway~

Riccardo, his initial skepticism giving way to genuine curiosity, found himself drawn into the unfolding drama.

As Anna set off on her journey and the complexities of the characters became more apparent, he abandoned his phone and focused solely on the screen.

His brows furrowed, as he saw Olaf.

It's like a little baby unicorn.

Wha ! Hey ! Woah !

Oh, I love it even more.

"Wow. A talking Snowman ?" Riccardo muttered.

"Ahh yeah, he is the best, Ric. Olaf is hilarious, just wait. He adds a lot to the story." Bella grinned.

Riccardo nodded his head again focusing on the walking and talking Snowman.

Hi everyone, I'm Olaf, and I like warm hugs !

A giggle left Bella's mouth as Olaf called Sven a 'Funky looking Donkey.'

She laughed out loud when he says that Sven is trying to kiss his nose. Riccardo let out a chuckle.

As the movie continues, Riccardo's interest grew as he find himself more engrossed in movie.

During the climactic scenes, especially when Anna sacrificed herself for Elsa, Riccardo's narrowed eyes had widened, fully engaged in the unexpected depth of the story.

The unexpected depth of the story caught him off guard.

"But why did Anna sacrifice herself ?"

He narrowed his eyes.

Bella smiled at him.

"It's about true love, Ric. She did it to save her sister, Elsa. It's beautiful."

"Beautiful ? It's literally a heartbreaking. Oh God, I thought it will be all cartoons, barbies, singing animals and happy endings. What is this ?" He exaggerate, still in slight shock.

According to him, Disney movies are Barbie movies.

Bella laughed at that.

"Nuh-uh Ric, Time has changed. This movie is all about sacrifice. Putting others first"

Riccardo narrowed his eyes at her.

"Oo so you are learning all these big words from these types of movies, aren't you ?"

She laughed at that.

"Ok, but on serious note, they shouldn't make it so intense. I mean can't they just break the curse with a true love's kiss or something ?"

"That's too cliché. This way, it's more real, more emotional. Anna's sacrifice adds depth to the story" Bella answered.

"But I just want to watch something light-hearted. This is just breaking my heart" He slightly argued.

"What is breaking your heart, Ric ?" A voice interrupts them. They looked up only to see Vincenzo there in casual clothes.

"Vinnyyyy" Bella ran towards Vincenzo who chuckled and immediately embraced her in his hold.

He picked her up and came towards Riccardo and sit beside him.

"So, what are you guys discussing ?" He looked at them with curiosity.

"N-Nothing" Riccardo immediately denied with slightly red ears.

Vincenzo narrowed his eyes and looked at Bella.

She laughed and said "Ric is sad"

"Why ?"

"Because Anna sacrifice herself for Elsa"

Vincenzo looked at her and then at Riccardo.

"Of course I will be sad. I thought they will end up with kissing and anything- why this has to be so intense" Riccardo grumbled.

Bella laughed at that while Vincenzo looked amused with his youngest brother behaviour.

<<°>>~<<°>>

"Who is Elsa though ?"

Bella's head snapped towards the owner of the voice. Her eyes widened in disbelief as well as shock.

Is this even possible ?

How could someone say like this ?

"How dare you ?" Two voices said together.

Matteo raised his eyebrow at both of them.

"I can't believe this, Teo. You don't know who is Elsa ? That means you also don't know about Anna, Olaf or anyone ?" Marco asked with wide eyes.

Bella gasped.

He narrowed his eyes and slightly shook his head.

"Oh My God, that's crime. We were bestfriends for so long and you are telling me this now ? Literally ? I can't believe you. You should know about Anna, Elsa and everyone else. Oh God, you are really living under rock" Marco exaggerate, keeping his both hands on his head.

Bella slightly giggled at his dramatics but decide to play along.

"Ok wait, who are these guys ?" He looked at both of them.

Bella sighed.

"Frozen movie characters" She replied.

"Oh" He rolled his eyes.

"Don't roll your eyes, Teo. You are going to watch Frozen and Frozen 2 today itself or else you are going to face me tomorrow" Marco warned.

Matteo looked at him in disbelief.

"Oh I am serious" He glared at him.

"Ok ok, chill" Matteo sighed.

Bella looked at them in amusement.

Bella has always been a bit reserved at school. It's not that she doesn't like having friends, but Bella has always preferred having a close-knit circle of friends. However, in her last school, she ended up being friend of some popular girls, who were only interested in superficial friendships. As an introvert, Bella loves to spend time alone. In fact, everyone values their privacy, but those friends of Bella didn't seem to understand the concept of privacy. According to them, only those who talk all day long are considered friends, which led Bella to start preferring to spend time alone.

When she joined this new school, the desire for a good circle of friends resurfaced in her mind. However, due to Alberto, she decided to stay alone again, thinking that the fault is not with anyone else but herself, that she couldn't get along with anyone. But ever since she met these two boys, there is once again hope for a good friendship in her mind.

She had never thought that the two boys she disliked from the very first day of school would be the ones to protect her, and now they are such good friends. She used to think that they would be typical bad boys, but she had never thought that they would be such kind-hearted boys.

"Earth to Bellaaa" She snapped out from her thoughts when she saw Marco is waving his hand infront of her eyes.

"Huh ?" She looked at them only to see Matteo's worried glance and Marco's confusing ones.

"Are you ok ?" Matteo asked.

"Yes. Why ?" She asked.

"We were calling you from last 92 seconds but you were not responding" Marco shrugged.

"Oh yeah, I was just thinking something" She replied.

"What ?" Matteo raised his eyebrow.

"How come you don't know about Elsa-"

"Heyyy Enough guys" Matteo almost whinned.

Marco and Bella laughed out loud, with high-five.

<<°>>~<<°>>

As the school day came to an end, the hallways echoed with the shuffling of feet and the chatter of students, the corridors became a bustling thoroughfare of students, their laughter and conversations filling the air.

Bella, shouldering her backpack, joined the flow of students heading toward the parking lot.

Marco and Matteo were already gone.

As Bella neared the entrance to the parking lot, she inadvertently crossed paths with a group of girls. Their laughter abruptly ceased, replaced by sharp glares that bore into Bella like icy daggers.

The ringleader, a girl with a haughty demeanor, sneered, "Watch where you're going, little girl"

Bella, taken aback, stammered an apology, "Sorry, I didn't mean to-"

"Your sorry won't fix this" Another girl from whom Bella actually bumped, said with irritation.

"Look what you have done. Because of you, my shoes are ruined" That girl gritted her teeth.

Bella frowned and looked down at her shoes. There is not a single trace of dirt on her shoes.

"But, I didn't step on it-"

"So now you are accusing me too ?" That girl glared at her.

Bella's lips parted as she immediately shook her head.

"I-I just... just-"

"You just what ? First, you bumped into me, then you stepped on my expensive shoes and now you are saying that I am lying ? Ridiculous. Do you have any manner ? Any shame ?" That girl yelled on Bella's face.

Bella looked at her in shock and disbelief. But before she could say anything, another girl cuts her off.

"Heyy, you are Bella Russo, right ?" A girl with red hair narrowed her eyes.

Bella nodded, suspiciously.

She chuckled and looked at her friends.

"Guys, leave her."

Bella inwardly sighed, mentally thanking her saviour. A small smile graced on her pink lips.

But that smile again disappeared when she heard the next words of that girl.

Bella's breath hitched as her eyes immediately welled up.

"Guys, forgive her. Of course, she is a mannerless, after all, she has no mother who could teach her manners."

To Be Continued...

Share your thoughts .

Don't forget to Vote and Comment.

I will meet you guys soon till then stay safe, take care and Love yourself .

Byee Byee ... Luv ya .

Published : 19 November 2023

Total words : 2032 words .

Chapter 18

"Guys, forgive her. Of course, she is a mannerless, after all, she has no mother who could teach her manners."

Bella's eyes widened.

"Ok, that could explain her this behaviour" Another girl with short hair said and they all laughed at that except the girl with whom she bumped. She is just plainly glaring at Bella.

"Even if she is motherless, do I look like I care ? You bitch, listen to me, I want my money" That girl said taking a step towards Bella.

Before Bella could say anything, first girl butts in, "Oh little girl, you never told us, where are your parents, huh ?"

"Did they leave you or they are just died ?"

Bella's head snapped towards the girl.

Her eyes glistened with tears.

Never in her life she expected she would face this.

"No guys, I think she is illegitimate"

Bella didn't know what that's mean. But judging from their laughing faces, she knew it is a bad word.

"Aww look, she is crying. Little Bella, don't cry, your Mom Dad will scold us", She shuddered fakely, "Oops, you don't have Mom-dad. Sorry"

They laughed at that.

Bella looked down feeling helpless first time in her life.

"See, little girl, our Mom and Dad came to pick us up. Who is coming to pick you up huh ?"

Bella bits her lips, looking down. Her eyes are just glistening more.

She so badly wants to reply them but she don't know what she will gonna reply them.

Their words pierced thorough her pure heart, shattering it into million pieces.

"Leave it guys, I am not in mood. You bitch, you tell me, when are you going to give me Money as you clearly ruined my expensive shoes" That girl gritted her teeth but immediately froze when she heard another voice.

"How much ?" Bella's head snapped towards that direction.

Her eyes sparkled seeing Vincenzo there.

While on another hand, all of them were froze on their places. Their eyes widened like a saucer, and mouth gaped open.

Vincenzo looked at them coldly.

He came towards them and kept his hand on Bella's shoulder, pulling her in his embrace, side-hugging her.

"Are you ok ?" He asked her softly.

She meekly nodded.

"Go sit in the car, I am coming"

He doesn't need to tell her twice. She immediately left from there. He turned towards the girls.

"So, what were you saying ?" Vincenzo asked coldly.

All of them gulped visibly.

"I-I - " She cleared her throat, "She ruined my e-expensive shoes. She need to pay."

That girl said mustering courage.

Vincenzo looked at her shoes and then at her face.

He took out his wallet and immediately gave her the money.

"It is more than your all of your Fathers' salary combined. Take this money, get a spectacles for yourselves. Because I don't think so there is a dirt anywhere."

They all looked down, totally embarassed.

"And one more thing, you are kids that's why I am not saying anything. But, if I ever heard any of you saying anything to my Sister, I will personally deal with you all. Don't forget, if I can give you the money more than your Fathers' salary then, I can also snatch your Fathers' jobs and make you homeless."

He warned them and left from there.

Yes, Vincenzo Russo is the Ruthless man. He doesn't care if the girls infront of him are kids or not. If anyone messes with his family then he is not going to leave them. Doesn't matter who is infront of him. He is only soft for his precious daughter and brothers. No one can mess with them. And he will take care of it.

They stood there froze and stiffened. Eyes widened like plate.

Vincenzo wore his shades and left from there.

He came towards his car and sat on the backseat.

Vincenzo was waiting for Bella as he came to pick her up from her school. But, as she was late, he decided to check in the school. And when he came there, his blood boiled when he heard what that girl is saying to his Bella. 'You bitch, you tell me, when are you going to give me Money as you clearly ruined my expensive shoes'.

How dare she to call his daughter a name ? He so badly wanted to bash her head on the wall.

But he controlled himself there.

Now, he could clearly see that Bella is somewhat silent.

Now don't get me wrong, Bella is actually silent and shy girl but she is never silent infront of her brothers.

"Baby, what happened ?" He asked her softly, caressing her hair.

She was looking outside the window, lost in her thoughts.

She flinched when she suddenly felt a touch on her head.

She looked towards Vincenzo.

"Bells, don't worry. I took care of those girls. They will never gonna bother you again. Don't worry, sweetheart" Vincenzo reassured her.

She nodded with a half smile on her face.

Vincenzo frowned at that.

"What happened ? What are you thinking Bella ?"

Bella looked at him with doe eyes.

Without thinking twice, she asked him, "Vinny, What is i-illegitimate ?"

Vincenzo's heart dropped.

Never in a million years could he have imagined that his Bella would ever ask about this.

He frowned.

"What ? Where did you hear this word ?" He asked her, sternly.

Bella's eyes glistened.

"Vinny, they called me illegitimate. I don't know what that means but I don't like it." She replied in a low voice, trying to stop the sob that is willing to left her mouth.

Vincenzo's jaw clenched. His eyes widened as his heart sank.

"V-Vinny, you know they told me that I am mannerless because I am orphan. Tell me, Vinny, am I m-mannerless ?" She looked in his eyes with tears streaming down her cheeks.

Vincenzo without a second thought, immediately shook his head.

"No Baby, they are lying. You are not mannerless, Bells. You are the most well mannered girl, I ever saw in my whole life, princess" He cupped her face and made her look at him.

"But they are right about one thing, Vinny. I am orphan. I am motherless child, Vinny" Her lips twitched downward as she cried.

"Bella" He immediately took her on his lap as he pushed her head in his chest.

"V-Vinny they c-called me motherless child- w-why Vinny ? Where is my Mom, Vinny ? Why don't I have a mother like other children, Vinny ? Is s-she angry on me ? P-Please tell her I will be good, please tell her to come to me. Why did she left me ? Am I that b-bad, D-Dada ? Please bring her, Please Dada. I also want my Mom. I also want her to drop me to school, to pick me up from school, to attend my PTM like other students' parents, Vinny, please bring her to me, P-Ple-ease I n-need her, Dada, I need her" She cried uncontrollably, saying things, which unknowingly is breaking Vincenzo's heart.

His heart shattered when he heard her saying She needs her, Mom.

He remembered Shaira saying that A girl needs her mother.

A lone tear escaped his eye, as he kept his daughter close to his heart tightly and caressed her hair, trying to calm her and himself.

He shut his eyes as he remember everything.

His past.

That Night.

That moment.

His Helplessness.

His tears.

His Beggings.

Those people.

Each and every thing. He couldn't understand one thing, in all these things,

What is Bella's fault in this ?

Why is she suffering ?

Why is she crying ?

Why is he always helpless ?

He is worthless if his daughter still misses her Mom.

He failed.

He failed as a father.

Time to think of it, he is always failure. Always. Failed as a son. Failed as a brother. Failed as a Father. Failure. Nothing but A big Failure.

He snapped out of his trance when driver said, "Sir, we are here"

He looked down only to see Bella slept in his embrace, fisting his shirt in her tight hold.

He sighed as he picked her up and took her to her room. He took out her shoes and socks and tucked her in. He sighed when he saw dried tears on her cheeks. He leaned in and kissed her forehead and immediately left from there.

Vincenzo entered his room with a heavy sigh, the weight of the day lingering in the air. Slowly, he loosened his tie, the knot giving way to the release of tension. His fingers moved deliberately, unbuttoning his shirt with a sense of weariness.

In the dimly lit room, shadows played on the walls as Vincenzo moved with a heavy heart. From a hidden corner, he retrieved a bottle.

The sound of the cork being reluctantly released echoed in the stillness, a prelude to the pouring of the crimson elixir into a crystal glass. Each drop fell with a melancholic grace, a testament to the weight of the thoughts that burdened his mind.

As he sat on the edge of the bed, the room seemed to absorb the silence.

As he brought the glass to his lips, the room seemed to hold its breath. Vincenzo sipped the wine slowly, savoring its bitter-sweet taste as if trying to drown the bitterness of the memories that haunted him. The liquid warmth provided a fleeting comfort, but the darkness in his eyes betrayed the turmoil within.

Bella's words echoed in his mind.

What is i-illegitimate, Vinny ?

They called me mannerless because I am orphan.

Am I that b-bad ?

Why did she left me ?

Please bring her to me, Vinny.

I need her.

Shaira's words played in his mind.

A daughter always needs her mother.

Seated on the edge of despair, Vincenzo stared into the void, the glass now a fragile vessel clutched tightly in his hands.

The silence of the room embraced him, echoing the silence he had faced in Bella's tears. The recollection of her cries resonated in his mind. The echo of her pleas for her mother reverberated, a haunting melody that refused to fade.

A mother.

A pure word. A singular syllable that resonates with purity and depth. In its simplicity, it encapsulates a universe of selfless love, boundless nurturing, and unwavering devotion. This word stands as a testament to the purity of a connection that goes beyond language, a primal chord that echoes through the human experience.

Those people are very lucky who have a mother.

But, what about his Bella ?

Why isn't she lucky ?

What will he say to her ?

How will he bring her mother to her ?

That mother, who left her own child to die as soon as she was born ?

That mother who is only concerned with money ?

That mother who gave nothing but trouble to her own daughter ?

He glared at nothing. His eyes darkened as the past unfolded before him.

Lost in the labyrinth of his thoughts, he didn't notice the glass crushed between his fingers, piercing into his skin. But the pain went unnoticed as he was ensnared in the depths of his grief.

His gaze, distant and glazed, remained fixed on the void before him, lost in the labyrinth of his own anguish.

His palms stained with the palette of his own suffering, Vincenzo remained oblivious to the blood seeping through the crevices between his fingers.

The physical pain seemed inconsequential, a mere whisper against the roar of his internal turmoil.

"Vince, that file-" Salvatore's eyes grew into wide-eyed as he beheld the scene before him. He gasped when he saw crimson liquid in his elder brother's fingers.

The sharp difference between the red blood and the pale color of Vincenzo's hands caught Salvatore off guard, leaving him breathless.

Without a second thought, he rushed towards his brother, "What the fuck, Vince ? What are you doing ? Leave it." Salvatore yelled at him, immediately taking actions.

He immediately took a first aid box from the drawer and sat beside him on the bed.

He took his hand and carefully removed the shard from his hand.

Salvatore's hands moved with a mix of precision and concern, delicately probing to extract the glass from Vincenzo's palm.

He frowned deeply seeing blood ozing out from his brother's hands.

"Are you out of your Mind ? What are you even thinking, Vincenzo ?" He scolded him, mending his wound.

However, Vincenzo remained an enigmatic figure, a statue of stoicism amid the storm of emotions. Just sitting there, emotionlessly. Without any pounce of expression, he just sat there numb.

Salvatore looked up frustrated.

"I am asking something. For God sake, reply me" Salvatore yelled at him, totally frustrated.

Vincenzo looked in his eyes.

"She needs her mother"

Salvatore frowned at that. But as realisation hits him hard, his eyes widened.

"What ?"

Vincenzo nodded.

"You know Sal, what she told me today ? She told me to bring her Mom. I don't know what to reply, Sal. I was speechless there. Tell me, Sal, from where I will bring her Mom ? How could I even fulfill her this wish ?" Vincenzo's eyes teared up.

Salvatore's heart sank seeing tears in his Elder brother's eyes.

"Today some girls called her illegitimate. Why ? What harm has she done to anyone ? She doesn't even know the meaning, Sal. I-I- she asked me that meaning. I-I was s-speechless- Sal" He couldn't help but, tears started streaming down his cheeks.

"I-If she needs her mother, that means I am failed-"

Salvatore immediately pulled him in a hug.

"Ssshh Shhh Calm down, Vince, you are not a failure-"

"No Sal. I am. You know, Sal, when I first held Bella in my arms, I made a promise to myself that come what may, I'll never let tears fill her eyes. I'll fulfill all her wishes, keep her happy always, and never let her feel the absence of her mother. Today, I lost, Sal, today I lost. M-My heart b-broke for her- she cried h-helplessly infront of me and I-I can't do a t-thing- she kept asking me that if her mom left her b-because she is mannerless or bad- I so badly wants to tell her that she is not bad. But- I can't- she told me that they called her o-orphan,-" Vincenzo pulled out from the hug and looked at Salvatore.

"-I-I want to tell her that s-she is not o-orphan, I am her Dad, I am her father. She is my child. M-My daughter. My kid." Salvatore's heart shattered when he saw Vincenzo gasped for a breath.

"S-She called me Dada Sal, I-I- I know she doesn't even realise that- I felt so helpless, Sal- My daughter thinks herself as an Orphan and I can't even tell her that I am her f-father- I am u-unlucky- I have a daughter and I can't even call her My daughter." Vincenzo cried uncontrollably.

Salvatore's tears rolled down his cheeks.

He let him cry. He let him to all out.

But now it is enough.

"Vince, you are not an unlucky. You have Bella as your daughter. You are the luckiest Dad ever. Did you realise, she cried for her Mom, not for her Dad, right ? That's because she got you. That's because, she saw her Dad in you. Do you forget her first PTM, Vince ? When she told you that you are her Dad. Remember ? You were on cloud nine that day, weren't you ? Vince, listen to me, hmm. It happens. She is kid. Kids often remember their parents. Do you forget how Ric used to remember them ? He got over it, right ? You know Vince, our Bella loves you so much. She doesn't need any mom or any other female figure in her life. She loves you and you are way more than enough for her. And, I promise you, Vince, that she will tell you this herself one day."

To Be Continued...

Hope you guys like it. I actually tried to write something emotional.

Share your thoughts about this chapter.

Don't forget to Vote and Comment.

I will meet you guys soon till then stay safe, take care and Love yourself .

Byee Byee ... Luv ya .

Published : 27 November 2023.

Total words : 2735 words .

Chapter 19

Vincenzo : 20 Years OldSalvatore : 18 Years OldRiccardo : 16 Years OldBella : 6 Years Old

"So, we have PTM tomorrow at 9:00 am. Every parent should be present there, ok ?"

A chorus of yes's heard.

Whispers and giggles fill the room as teacher left the class.

"I will bring my Mommy, tomorrow, because My Daddy is busy" One little girl said to her friends.

"Ohh, I will bring my Mom, too. Because my Daddy is in America" Another boy said.

"Ha ha ha, My Daddy is never busy for me, so he will come tomorrow." A girl smirked.

"My Dad is not busy but I am scared because what if he will come to know about my marks." Another Boy shuddered at the thought.

"Oh I forgot about it. My parents are very strict." Girl widened her eyes.

"Same" Another one gasped.

"I am lucky here. My parents never scold me" A boy said proudly.

"Nuh-uh my Mom scold me, but my Daddy always protect me from my Mom" A little girl grinned cheekily.

"What about you, Bella ? Who is going to come with you ? Your Mom or Dad ?" A girl asked curiously.

Bella shrugged her shoulders "My Brother"

All of them frowned at that.

PTM means Parents Teachers Meeting, right ? Then Why brother ?

"Ohh but I don't think so teacher will allow you to bring your brother. It's parents teachers meeting, Dumbo" A boy replied laughing.

Bella frowned at that.

Vinny will take care of it, right ?

Of course, he will.

"Ok leave it. Bella, I never saw your parents. Tell us about them. Are your parents also strict ?" Another girl asked her.

Bella shrugged, finding herself speechless.

"She doesn't have parents" A new voice chimmed in.

Bella looked at the boy who just arrived there.

All of them gasped at that.

"You are lying." A Girl accused that boy.

"I am not lying. Ask her, if you are thinking I am lying." That boy shrugged his shoulders.

Every attention turned towards Bella.

Bella looked down.

"B-But how is it possible ?" One girl stuttered.

"Why ?"

"What do you mean why ? There are no children without parents. Bella would not have been born if she had not had parents." That girl whispered her theory to the group.

They gasped at that.

Bella's frown deepened.

"Who told you this ?" Another girl asked her.

"My Sister" She replied.

"Ohh, then, I guess, her parents left her." That Boy smirked.

"Yes, that's possible. My Daddy said that if I bother someone, they will leave me."

"That means Bella bothered them, that's why they left her."

"Bella, you shouldn't bother your parents."

"Yes, now see they left you."

A girl gasped "That means, she will never get to see her parents ?"

All of them shook their heads in denial.

Bella's eyes glistened.

"She is unlucky. She will never get her Daddy's and Mommy's love like us."

"Yes, My Daddy loves me so much. He brings me everything. He is little busy but whenever he gets time, he played with me, he gives me everything."

"Yepp, My Daddy is very strict. He scolds me, whenever I bother him but he never left me. Poor Bella."

"Her Mommy left her too. Bella, you are literally bothersome, huh ?"

"Yes, What if your brothers also got fed up with you and left you ?"

Bella's head snapped towards them.

She can't live without her brothers.

"Then, she will live in Orphanage"

They laughed at that.

Bella bit her lips and shut her eyes tightly.

"What is happening here ? Sit on your seats, quickly." A teacher shouted on everyone.

They immediately scattered and sat on their respective seats and the class started.

<<°>>~<<°>>

"What happened Babes ? What's going on in your little mind ?"

It's evening. No one is at home except Salvatore and Bella. From the time, she came from school, he noticed something is definitely wrong. Because the always chatterbox Bella is silent today.

Bella looked at him and pouted.

He chuckled and squeezed her cheeks.

For him, she is the cutest little thing. He just want to put her in his pocket.

""Do I really bother you all that much ?" She asked showing her puppy dog eyes.

He frowned. He didn't expect this question.

Nonetheless, he made a thinking face.

"Ummm not that much but yeah" He answered playfully.

She gasped.

"Then, are you really going to leave me ?" Her eyes widened in shock.

Salvatore's frown deepened.

But before he could say anything,

"Nooooo Sally, please don't leave me. I don't want to live in Orphanage. I will miss you guys there. Mom and Dad also left me because I was a bother to them. I swear I will be a good kid. You will never get my complaint. I will wake up on time, eat my breakfast like a good kid, will go to school everyday and complete my homework too. Just please don't leave me. If you will tell me, I will not play at all- n-no wait- I will play only a little, not much. Because, playing is necessary for kids, and I am also kid. Please, promise me, you guys will never leave me. Please Sallyyy, please promise me, please, please-"

Salvatore just looked at her with wide amused eyes.

He immediately pulled her in his lap and hugged her.

"Why would we leave you ?" Salvatore asked her softly.

"Because, I bother you a lot." She mumbled.

"So ?"

"So, you guys will leave me in Orphanage."

"No Babes, we would never. You know, Ric is naughtier than you. Do you even know Do you even know the level of trouble he has caused us ? You are literally nothing infront of him. That boy is a walking bomb. You know, he once put pink colour in my hair dye. I literally roam around in pink colour. It was so embarassing." Salvatore told her.

She gasped at the newfound information.

"This is nothing. You know, one day that boy put a toothpaste in oreo biscuit."

She frowned.

"He ate all the cream of the biscuit and replaced that cream with tooth-paste. And we were prey of his pranks." He sighed.

Bella's eyes widened. Her jaw dropped.

"He was naughty" she mumbled.

"Was ? He is Bella, He is." Salvatore scoffed.

Bella giggled.

"So should we leave him in the orphanage ?" He asked her.

Bella's head snapped towards him. She immediately shook her head.

"No Sally, we can't. He will be sad there" She pouted.

Salvatore chuckled.

"Then why did you think that we will leave you in the orphanage ?" He asked her, caressing her hair.

"My friends told me" She pouted.

"What ?"

"That I-I- am not good girl that's why M-Mommy and Daddy left me and you guys will too, if I will bother you" She mumbled.

Salvatore's heart clenched for the little girl.

She is just a kid.

"Babes, no one is going to leave you. I swear. Your friends don't know how much we love our Bella." He hugged her close to his heart.

"But, Sally, Mom Dad did. They left." Her eyes glistened with tears breaking Salvatore's heart.

"No Bells, they didn't. Ok, tell me, What do fathers do for their children ?" He asked her.

She thought for a moment, "Fathers love their Children. My friend Anna told me her daddy always tuck her in, he always gave her ice-cream whenever she is upset, he attends her PTM, he always gave her gifts when she will get good marks, he always throws a party on her birthday, he woke her up with kisses and hugs, sometimes he even feeds her. You know, Sally, they told me I can't have Mommy's and Daddy's love" She said with teary eyes.

"They are lying, Baby. If Anna's dad tucks in her, then your Vinny also tucks you in. Tell me, whenever you feel sad, what does Vinny do ?" He asked her wiping her tears.

"He always bakes for me, because he knows how much I like sweets, he also gives me ice cream and chocolates." Bella replied.

"Who attends your PTM ?"

"Vinny"

"Tell me, does Vinay ever scold you for scoring less marks ?" He asked her.

She immediately shook her head.

"No, never. Vinny never scolds me. Whether I score well or not, he always gives me gifts. He always says that for him my scores do not matter, what matters is only my efforts." Bella replied.

Salvatore smiled at that.

"Now tell me love, Why do you feel that you do not get your father's love, hmm ?" He asked her softly.

Bella tilted her head.

He is right.

Vinny loves her sooo much that for her, he is not only her brother but a father figure. He gives her the love that a father should give to their children. He hugs her when she was scared. He comforts her when she was sad. He was there for her when she needed him.

Bella is only 6 years old. But she knew that, she can't live without her Vinny.

But when Sally told her everything, she realised she actually never missed any father figure in her life. She always has father in her eldest brother. She never missed her father. She just get manipulated by those students' words.

She has Vinny. She doesn't need anyone else.

"You are right, Sally. I have Vinny. I don't need anyone else." She sniffled, immediately hugging him.

He hugged her back tightly.

Caressing her head, he continued, "Never think about anything negative, Babes. You are never a bad kid. Nobody is going to leave you just because you are naughty. We need our Naughty Bella in our life and we are NEVER going to leave you. I promise."

Bella looked up from his chest, looking at him with her doe eyes.

"Sally"

"Hmm ?" He looked down at her.

She looked so cute.

He immediately leaned in and kissed on her forehead and nose.

"So why did Mommy leave me ?"

Salvatore stiffened at that.

He looked at her. His eyes softened at the innocence in her eyes.

What will he say to her now ? He can neither lie nor tell the truth. Neither can he say that her mother has died nor can he say that her mother does not even like to see her face. That little girl would be devastated if she came to know the truth about her mother.

He cupped her face and stared in his eyes.

"Some people needs to leave, Bella and it's for the good."

Bella didn't understand that but didn't question either.

She just leaned on his chest.

<<°>>~<<°>>

"Good Night, love" Vincenzo kissed on her forehead and was going to left.

Before he could even stand, he felt a tug.

He looked back and frowned.

"What happened, Baby ?"

Bella sighed and got up from the bed.

She jumped on him and he immediately caught her in his arms.

"Are you ok ? What happened ?" He asked her, holding her comfortably in his hold.

"Can I cuddle with you today ?" She mumbled on his shoulder.

He slightly frowned at the tone but nodded nonetheless.

"Sure, let's go" He took her in his bedroom and they cuddled.

He made her sleep on the bed and went to washroom.

He did his business and sat on the bed.

Bella immediately put her one arm around his chest. Her little arm couldn't even reach to his other side. She put her little leg on his stomach.

Vincenzo chuckled at his clingy baby.

"Now tell Vinny what happened ?"

Without any second thought, she blurted out.

"You are my Dad."

Vincenzo stiffened at that. His heartbeat skipped as his eyes slightly widened.

"Vinny, I am so happy that I have you." She grinned and kissed his cheek.

Gulping a lump in his throat, he asked "What actually happened ?"

And there she told him everything.

His heart clenched for the little girl. She is suffering.

"Vinny, you are the best. Other students parents scold them when they get less marks but you never scold me. Their fathers are always busy in their work but you were never busy for me. Their fathers don't know how to cook, but you know everything. From cooking to baking. Everything. Their fathers are their heros. But You are MY superhero, Vinny. I don't need Dad, when I have you, Vinny. I love you so much"

Vincenzo's eyes teared.

He never expect this from his 6 year old.

The girl who don't even know the world, knows so much about her Vinny. The girl who sometimes can't even make proper sentence, tell such a deep thing.

Vincenzo was over the moon. His heart bloomed with happiness as his eyes glistened more.

He immediately pulled her in his embrace. She hugged him back.

He was speechless.

He don't know how to express anything. But he knows one thing that he is the luckiest and happiest father of the world.

"Still, Riccy is my favourite." She muttered.

Vincenzo frowned and pulled out from the hug. He narrowed his eyes at her. She cutely smirked at him.

"You brat-" He said and tickled her.

She laughed out loudly.

That night, both of them sleep peacefully with a content smile on their face.

Vincenzo never asked for more. He was overjoyed.

His daughter called him her father.

He was more than happy.

He tightly hugged his treasure close to his heart and kissed her head.

"Never let it change, please."

To Be Continued...

Sorry, I don't know what I had actually written here. In my Defence, I am on my Periods. First Day.

Tell me if you want to read anything specific... I mean any request or any particular scene ?

Please tell me if there is any mistake or if you feel that this is boring or something like that.

Or

Appreciate me if it is good lol .

Don't forget to Vote and Comment.

I will meet you guys soon till then stay safe, take care and Love yourself .

Byee Byee ... Luv ya .

Published : 3 December 2023.

Total words : 2351 words .

Chapter 20

As the sun begins its descent, casting a tapestry of warm hues across the sky, Bella stirs from her slumber.

The room is bathed in the soft, amber glow of the sunset, and the delicate curtains dance with the gentle evening breeze.

She slowly opened her eyes, with a yawn. Her hands rubbing her sleep from her eyes.

Her gaze drifts across the room with a confusion flicker in her eyes.

"I was in car" She mumbled remembering the moment before she slept.

It must be Vinny, who carried her here.

A sigh left her mouth remembering the incident happened in the school.

Those Girls.

Orphan.

Mannerless.

Bitch.

Motherless child.

Her eyes teared up as their cruel words echoed in her innocent mind.

She immediately wiped her tears and looked at her clock.

She sighed and untangled herself from blankets seeing the clock strike 4:45 pm.

She wore her slippers and move towards her washroom. After completing her business, she came downstairs feeling a bitter silence in her home.

"I am hungry" She mumbled. Rubbing her stomach, she went towards the kitchen.

Her eyes fell on her two younger older brothers.

"Nah ! I am free today, why ?" Riccardo replied.

"Bec-"

"Sally" Their heads snapped towards the source of the voice.

Salvatore's eyes softened seeing her red puffy eyes.

He opened his arms and she immediately ran towards his embrace. He picked her up tightly hugging her to his chest.

Oh ! How much he loves this girl !

She snuggled in his embrace like a kitten.

"You are actually a puppy smuggling in his Momma dog's embrace" Riccardo laughed.

A pair of glares thrown in his direction made him laugh more.

Ignoring him, Salvatore asked Bella softly, "Are you hungry ?"

She nodded her head, closing her eyes.

"Hey Hey, don't sleep or you will not gonna sleep at night." Salvatore said, gently shaking her.

"I am not sleeping just thinking something." She mumbled with still eyes closed.

"Huh then think with open eyes" He said, patting her cheeks.

She opened her eyes and glared at him.

"Sit here and I will make something for you" He said making her sit on the chair, beside Riccardo.

She kept her head down on the table.

"Bella, don't sleep." Salvatore said, going towards the refrigerator.

Riccardo smirked and pulled her hairtie making her high pony tail loose.

"So, tell me, what do you want to eat ?" Salvatore asked, looking in fridge.

She groaned and swatted his hand, "Anything is fine."

Riccardo again ruffled her hair.

She glared at him and smacked his arms.

"What about white sauce Pasta ?" He asked.

"Ok"

Riccardo pulled her hairtie out of her hair making her sighed in frustration.

"Sallyyyy, Riccyyy keeps pulling my hair" She let out a exhausted whin making Riccardo chuckle.

"Ric, don't pull her hair." Salvatore said sternly, meticulously taking out his ingredients - butter, all-purpose flour, milk, salt, pepper, and pasta.

"It's fun to wind her up" He replied, smirking.

Bella gave him dirty look trying to tie her hair in bun.

"Ignore him Bells, Tell me what you studied in school today ?" Salvatore asked her, purposely leaving the topic of what happened in school today instead he asked what she studied in school.

And as expected, she started telling him about her all subjects.

In a large pot of boiling water seasoned with salt, Salvatore cooked the pasta to al dente perfection. The kitchen filled with the comforting scent of simmering noodles.

"It smells so good" Bella grinned.

Salvatore winked at her.

"You know Sally, Mark and Matty loves your food especially Mark. He keeps telling me that he wants to be your brother so that he could eat everything this tasty, everytime." She giggled, remembering Marco's comments on Salvatore's food.

Salvatore chuckled at that.

In a separate saucepan, he melted a generous amount of butter over medium heat.

Riccardo scoffed at that, "Tell him that he is lucky to not get him as his brother" He grumbled, specifically pointing towards Salvatore, who in response plainly glared at him.

Bella frowned, "Why ?"

"Because ask his real brother how much this so called brother bothers him."
He rolled his eyes.

"Like you never bother him" Bella replied, squinting her eyes, defending
her Sally.

Salvatore chuckled. She definitely is his little lawyer.

Once melted, he added a precise measure of all-purpose flour, stirring
vigorously to create a smooth roux.

Riccardo scoffed at that.

"Leave him, Babes, why don't you invite them tomorrow at dinner ?"
Salvatore asked her, lowering the heat and pouring the milk gradually. He
seasoned the sauce with a pinch of salt and pepper.

Bella's eyes lit up.

"Really ?" She grinned.

"Yepp, of course, why not" He shrugged.

"Yes, to showoff his cooking" Riccardo mumbled under his breath, but
none of them heard or maybe choose to ignored him.

With the flame reduced, Salvatore let the sauce simmer gently, allowing it
to thicken to a creamy consistency. The kitchen filled with the rich aroma.

"Bells, go and wake Vince till then it will be ready."

Bella nodded and immediately left from there.

"So, Is Vince going to complain to principal about those girls ?" Riccardo
asked him, seriously.

The mischief glint from his eyes were gone.

Salvatore sighed.

"I don't know. He was not actually in sense then. He kept telling me that how he failed to raise her."

Once the pasta reached its al dente glory, Salvatore drained it and mixed it into the velvety white sauce, ensuring every strand was coated in the luscious concoction.

"What ? Is he out of his mind or what ? Those bitches-" Riccardo rubbed his temple in frustration.

"Control Ric. Those girls called Bella 'Bitch'. I don't want you to call them the same word infront of her. Understand ?" He stared at him, sternly, pointing his spoon infront of him.

Riccardo grumbled but nodded.

Salvatore plated the pasta, garnishing it with a sprinkle of freshly ground pepper and a touch of grated Parmesan.

Bella came running inside the kitchen.

"He woke up" She smiled sitting on her previous chair.

Salvatore smiled and said, "And your pasta is ready too"

With plates in hand, Salvatore sat across from his sister, giving both of his kids their plates.

With each bite, Bella's sleepiness waned, replaced by giggles and wide-eyed fascination as they talked about anything and everything.

Vincenzo entered in the kitchen quietly, the weight of previous incident etched on his face. However, as his eyes swept over the scene before him.

His Daughter engrossed in storytelling his brothers about something very interesting as her eyes widened in surprise, with a spark in it. While his brothers were listening it with so much interest, like it gives them the best happiness of the world.

A profound sense of relief washed over him.

A soft smile graced Vincenzo's lips, and his tired eyes sparkled with a mixture of gratitude and contentment. The knots of worry in his chest loosened as he witnessed the simple yet profound joy radiating from his family. The clinking of utensils and the laughter that echoed in the kitchen became a soothing melody, momentarily lifting the stress and tension that often rested on Vincenzo's shoulders.

<<°>>~<<°>>

The classroom hummed with the energetic buzz of students, each engrossed in their own world of chatter and laughter.

Bella, sat there with a girl, whose name is still unknown to her. She was busy in her own company, drawing something in her last page of her book.

Just as the lively banter reached its crescendo, the door swung open with a creak, drawing the attention of every student.

Mrs. Anderson.

Their Biology Teacher came inside with a beautiful smile graced on her face.

A hush fell over the room as all eyes turned towards her.

Mrs. Anderson stood at the front of the classroom, her eyes sparkling with enthusiasm as she announced, "Good afternoon, class! I have some thrilling news for all of you."

Each and every eyes grew wide with curiosity including Bella's.

Teacher smiled widely seeing the curiosity in every eyes.

"We are embarking on a four-day adventure to the enchanting forest re-serves next week!" A ripple of excitement surged through the room, punc-tuated by gasps and wide-eyed expressions.

She continued, "Our school organised this educational camp every year to teach us the importance of Environment as well as to teach us the components of Environment. We are going to live in tent there. We will learn how people who are residing in forest, are actually surviving there. We will do various activities like trecking, swimming etc."

The teacher continued, detailing the itinerary with vivid descriptions of wildlife, nature trails, and team-building activities.

Bella loves Nature. And trip to Nature is what she needs right now. Her eyes sparkled with excitement and enthusiasm.

"Living in forest means there will be Lizards and cockroaches. Ewww, I won't come." A girl screeched.

Mrs. Anderson smiled.

"No problem kid, Insects are also species. And we will ensure everyone's safety there so, it never be a problem. And one more thing, your seniors will also accompany you."

"Miss, how will we go to the camp from here ? I mean Mode of transporta-tion." A boy asked.

"School Bus" She told them.

"So those who are interested, I am distributing the consent forms. Fill it right now and bring tomorrow with your guardian's signature. Ok ?"

A chorus of yes's and ok's are heard.

She smiled, "Now, please take a moment to fill out these consent forms."

The rustling of papers echoed in the room as students eagerly scanned the details of the upcoming adventure. Mrs. Anderson, her tone both firm and cheerful, instructed, "Make sure your guardians sign these forms, granting permission for the trip. It's a wonderful opportunity, and I'm sure you wouldn't want to miss out."

With those words, Mrs. Anderson left the class buzzing with excitement.

Immediately packing her bag, she came out of her class in searching for her two friends.

Marco and Matteo.

She reached at their regular places, i.e. Terrace. She raised her eyebrows seeing both boys there.

"When did you guys come here ?" She asked them.

Matteo shrugged while Marco replied, "Just now."

Bella nodded.

"You guys will come to the camp, right ?" She asked them excitedly.

"That educational camp ?" Matteo asked.

She nodded, grinning.

"You wanna go ?" He asked further.

She immediately nodded.

"Same goes to me." Marco grinned too.

"Then, me too" Matteo shrugged.

Bella's eyes lit up.

"Now let's eat something, I am hungry." Marco grumbled.

Other two rolled their eyes, "You are always hungry."

Marco huffed at that.

"Guys, I forgot to tell you something." She immediately said.

"What ?"

"Sally invited you guys today" She grinned ear to ear.

"Really ? Sally's food ?" Marco's eyes lit up as he squealed happily.

Bella giggled at that while Matteo shook his head, amused.

<<°>>~<<°>>

"Please please please Vinny, I wanna go there" Bella pouted.

The living room echoed with the excitement of an impending adventure as Bella gave her the cutest look possible.

After coming back from school, she directly went to their office with the help of driver. To her surprise, Riccardo is also there instead of his college. With her excitement she told them about her camp. But, Vincenzo told her 'No' much to her dismay.

She was shocked at first as he never Denys her any request then what happened.

"Baby, it's not safe in forest." He tried to reason her. His voice held concern. His protective nature evident in the furrowed lines on his forehead.

"But Vinny, it's just a school camp for four days! I promise I'll be careful, and my teachers and even Matty and Mark will be there too," Bella pleaded, her voice tinged with excitement.

Vincenzo sighed, running a hand through his hair.

He don't want to make her sad but he just can't shake off that feeling.

"Vince is right. I don't think so, you should go there, Bella" Riccardo commented.

Bella frowned. Her lips turned downward.

"Please Riccy, please Vinny, I really want to go. They will do so many things there, please I don't want to miss all those." She pouted with a sad look on her face.

"Enough you guys, I don't think so there is any problem there. She will not alone there. There will be security, teachers infact Marco and Matteo are also going with her so, I think it's not an issue."

Salvatore voiced out his thoughts.

"That's the thing Sal, those boys are also there and I don't trust those boys. I am not letting her go with them." Riccardo grumbled.

"Shut up Ric, and Vince, I understand your worries but think, we can't keep her locked up forever. Besides, we'll send securities with them too."

He mumbled last part to Vincenzo as Bella is busy convincing Riccardo who keeps looking at her with a straight face.

Vincenzo looked at him with unsure gaze.

"That's not the thing, Sal, you know how Shaira is just waiting for us to make a single mistake. I don't want my daughter anywhere near that women." He muttered.

"Vince, that's what I am saying, we can't just keep her locked up forever just because that shitty excuse of woman is out there. We will send securities with the school. So, I don't think so, she will harm Bella anytime there." Salvatore looked confident.

Vincenzo still didn't look convince.

"Besides Vince, this is the best way to get her mind off that bullying thing. She will feel fresh and better. You know, how much she loved nature." Salvatore kept his hand on his brother's shoulder, squeezing it little.

"Vinny, tell him to stop bothering me" Bella whinned coming towards him.

"What did he do, Bella ?" Salvatore asked, smiling.

"He keeps telling me No again and again" She pouted.

"That's because you keep pestering me with your whinings and I am right you are not going anywhere." Riccardo huffed.

Before Bella could say anything, Salvatore interrupted.

"Ignore him, Bells, ask Vince, I am sure, he will agree. Show your secret weapon." He winked at her. A smile immediately came on her lips.

Bella seized the moment, intensifying her puppy dog eyes and throwing in a subtle pout.

"Vince, don't look at her." Riccardo warned.

"Shut up, Ric" Salvatore glared at him.

She scooted closer to him and looked at him with the most innocent and big doe eyes.

"Please please please Vinny, Everyone is going, It'll be so much fun and I'll be so sad if I can't join my friends. I really want to go."

Vincenzo sighed, torn between his protective instincts and his daughter's puppy dog eyes. Bella, sensing an opportunity, unleashed the full power of her pout.

"Come on, Vinny, please !" she pleaded, eyes widening and lower lip quivering just a bit.

"Ok, Ok, But you have to promise me you'll be cautious, Bella." He told her seriously and sternly.

Bella's face lit up with a victorious grin as she threw her arms around Vincenzo. "Thank you, thank you, thank you, Vinny ! You're the best big brother ever !"

He immediately caught her pulling her close.

Salvatore smiled widely while Riccardo looked at the scene in utter disbelief.

"You shouldn't let her, Vince with those boys-"

"Shut up, Ric" Three of them snapped at him.

"Rude" He muttered rolling his eyes.

<<°>>~<<°>>

"MARK, MATTY" Bella immediately ran towards the doors seeing her friends there.

"Bells" Marco grinned and hugged her. While, Matteo ruffled her hair.

"Enough hugging, princess." Riccardo pulled her out of their hold.

Marco huffed at that as he literally snatched her from his hug.

While Salvatore and Vincenzo rolled their eyes.

"Come inside kids" Salvatore welcome them with warm smiles.

"Thank you, Sir" They smiled back.

"Don't call us, Sir, kids. We are also like your brothers. Call us with our names." Vincenzo said with a smile.

"Brothers, my foot." Riccardo scoffed and mumbled inaudibly.

"Thanks Si-Vince" Matteo replied.

They came inside and talked for sometime more like Riccardo keeps interrogating them until Vincenzo warned him that he will really lock him inside his room. He stopped but nonetheless glared at them time to time. He actually don't like how Bella is getting close to them. Boys actually enjoyed there. They played many games and made jokes here and there.

"Nancy" Vincenzo called.

Nancy came there.

"Bring food for everyone and you eat too" He ordered.

Nancy smiled and nodded. She went in kitchen and bring food for everyone.

Their eyes went wide, seeing the number of dishes infront of them.

Dishes :-

1) Spaghetti Bolognese : Spaghetti Bolognese is an Italian pasta dish featuring a slow-cooked meat sauce with ground beef, tomatoes, onions, carrots, and herbs. Served over spaghetti, it's a classic comfort food, often garnished with Parmesan cheese.

2. Ravioli : Ravioli is Italian pasta with small dough pockets filled with ingredients like ricotta, spinach. Boiled and served with sauces, it's a versatile and popular dish.

3) Fettuccine alfredo : Fettuccine Alfredo is a classic Italian pasta dish featuring flat ribbon noodles (fettuccine) tossed in a creamy sauce made with butter, heavy cream, and grated Parmesan cheese. The result is a rich and indulgent pasta dish, often seasoned with salt, pepper, and sometimes nutmeg.

4) Lasagna Bolognese : Lasagna Bolognese is a variation of the classic Italian dish, featuring layers of wide pasta sheets, rich Bolognese sauce (made with ground meat, tomatoes, onions, and herbs), creamy béchamel sauce, and melted cheese. The result is a flavorful and satisfying baked casserole with a hearty meaty sauce.

5) Margherita Pizza : Margherita pizza is a classic variation topped with simple yet flavorful ingredients. It typically features a thin crust topped with fresh tomatoes, mozzarella cheese, fresh basil leaves, olive oil, and a sprinkle of salt. The colors of the toppings-red tomatoes, white mozzarella, and green basil-reflect the Italian flag, and it's named after Queen Margherita of Italy. The simplicity of ingredients highlights the freshness and quality of the pizza.

6) Arancini : Arancini are Italian rice balls that are typically filled, coated, and deep-fried. The name "arancini" means "little oranges" in Italian, likely due to their round and golden appearance. The most common filling is a mixture of rice, tomato sauce, mozzarella, and sometimes meat. These crispy and flavorful treats are enjoyed as a popular snack or appetizer in Italian cuisine.

7) Cannoli : Cannoli is indeed a sweet dish. It is a traditional Italian dessert that consists of tube-shaped pastry shells filled with a sweet and creamy ricotta cheese filling. The filling can also include ingredients like sugar,

vanilla, chocolate chips, or candied fruits. Cannoli are often enjoyed as a delicious treat and are a popular dessert in Italian cuisine.

8) Cassata Siciliana : Cassata Siciliana is a traditional Sicilian dessert known for its rich and indulgent flavors. It typically consists of a sponge cake or layers of sweetened ricotta cheese, candied fruit, and a layer of marzipan or icing. The cake is often soaked in liqueur, such as Marsala wine. Decorated with vibrant colors and intricate designs, Cassata Siciliana is a festive and visually appealing sweet treat enjoyed during special occasions and holidays in Sicily and beyond.

9) Panna Cotta : Panna Cotta is a classic Italian dessert that translates to "cooked cream." It is a simple and elegant dish made by simmering cream, sugar, and vanilla, then mixing it with gelatin to set. The result is a silky, custard-like dessert with a subtle vanilla flavor. Panna Cotta is often served chilled and can be accompanied by various toppings such as fruit coulis, caramel, or berries. Its smooth texture and versatility make it a popular and delightful treat in Italian cuisine.

10) Cioccolata Calda : Hot Chocolate

A/n : All these informations are from chatgpt and photos are from Pinterest.

"Oh My God" Marco mumbled looking at the delicious food items on the table. His mouth watered.

Same goes for Bella.

"When I asked you to make waffles for me, you straight forward denied me on my face, Sally." Riccardo looked at Salvatore in accusation.

Salvatore rolled his eyes at his little brother's childishness.

"First of all don't call me, that" He continue.

"About that, Because, that was 3:30 at night, Ric. You literally barged in my room and woke me up with not so gentleness and literally ordered me to make Waffles at that ungodly hour. What do you expect me to do ?" Salvatore replied, glaring at him.

Others laughed at that while Vincenzo bit his smile back.

Riccardo huffed, "That's not matter. Matter is you are unfair to me."

Salvatore again rolled his eyes.

"Eat kids" Vincenzo told them.

They digged in.

"It's so delicious, Sal." Marco grinned.

"Really, you like it ?" Salvatore asked with a smile.

"Yes, it's really nice." Matteo replied with a smile.

"Yepp, this is awesome, Sally. Bells always told us how you are the best cook ever. Your dishes are delicious. She always shares her food with me and from the time, I tasted your food, trust me, I am your biggest fan. And today, I literally loved it, Sally, thank you so much-"

Everyone looked at him with shock. He stopped himself when he saw how everyone is staring at him.

He awkwardly scratch his neck and laughed, "Sorry for the rant but, I really like your food."

He concluded it with a grin.

Everyone laughed at his antics.

"Thanks Kid, this really means a lot." Salvatore smiled, ruffling his hair with affection.

Riccardo scoffed.

"You don't mind of him calling you 'Sally'" He narrowed his eyes at his older brother.

Salvatore again rolled his eyes, but replied smirking,

"No"

Riccardo just plainly glared at him.

"Did you see that, Sally, I told you right How much they love your food ?" Bella grinned.

Marco and Matteo smiled and nodded.

"Yeah, actually, they love your food Sal." Vincenzo told him.

Salvatore threw a knowing wink at his direction to which Vincenzo rolled his eyes.

"You guys are lucky that he is not making you eat his green dishes" Vincenzo smirked, to which Salvatore frowned.

"What ?" Boys wondered.

"Yeah, his green dishes will include everything green like Broccoli, cabbage, spinach, bottle gourd and bitter gourd. His green drinks are also in green colour and that thing actually tastes like shit." Riccardo smirked.

Salvatore scoffed.

"That thing actually called as Bitter gourd juice. It is really beneficial for the body. It reduces several blood-sugar control markers, including hemoglobin A1c and fructosamine. It is a detoxifying agent which makes it quite beneficial for the liver. Besides, it reduces Body weight too, so, it's quiet beneficial for the body. You'll should drink that." Salvatore encouraged everyone.

"That's so good. I swear from tomorrow I will start drinking Bitter gourd juice everyday, Sally." Marco chimmed in with sparkle in his eyes.

Bella gasped.

"He became your fan, Sal. He will eat everything you will suggest." Matteo sighed.

Salvatore chuckled while Riccardo looked at him in disbelief.

Vincenzo smiled.

"That will be bitter, Mark" Bella told him, genuinely.

"It's ok, Bells. I could also maintain my body just like him. And you know, Sometimes to gain something you have to lose something, darling." Marco winked at her.

"Heyyy, stop. Don't call her that." Riccardo glared at him.

Vincenzo's smile also faltered for a second. Even Matteo narrowed his eyes at him.

While Salvatore sighed at his brothers' behaviour.

"They are kids, Ric" He reminded everyone.

Riccardo rolled his eyes.

"You guys are also going to camp, right ?" Vincenzo asked them, continue eating his food.

"Yes, Vince" Matteo nodded.

"I told you, Vinny that they are also coming. You know what Mrs.Ander son told us ?"

"What ?" He raised his eyebrows.

"That, we will also do trecking and swimming there and we will also live in tent-"

Like this, with laughter and smiles they spend their time, totally unaware of the storm that is waiting for them ahead.